A Candlelight Ecstasy Romance

"THAT WAS AN ASININE THING TO DO. YOU MIGHT HAVE BLOWN THE WHOLE DEAL!"

Sarah glared. "Don't be silly. Nobody saw."

"How do you know?" Tom demanded.

"I made sure nobody was looking."

"How can you tell with that many people around? Your coming up on the roof with me was to keep my men from finding out about my fear of heights. Don't you think it was just slightly dumb to grab my hand as if I were a five-year-old?"

Sarah was getting angry. What gave him the right to yell at her? "I was only giving moral support. You're acting as if I whipped a straitjacket out of my purse and put it on you."

"Don't give me that, Sarah. All I know is that now everyone'll think I'm scared to death—and they're right!"

CANDLELIGHT ECSTASY ROMANCES®

HEIGHTS
OF
DESIRE

Molly Katz

A CANDLELIGHT ECSTASY ROMANCE®

Published by
Dell Publishing Co., Inc.
1 Dag Hammarskjold Plaza
New York, New York 10017

Dell ® TM 681510, Dell Publishing Co., Inc.

Candlelight Ecstasy Romance®, 1,203,540, is a registered
trademark of Dell Publishing Co., Inc., New York,
New York.

ISBN: 0-440-13615-6

Printed in the United States of America

First printing—February 1986

For John Collins,
the best, with heartfelt thanks

To Our Readers:

We have been delighted with your enthusiastic response to Candlelight Ecstasy Romances®, and we thank you for the interest you have shown in this exciting series.

In the upcoming months we will continue to present the distinctive sensuous love stories you have come to expect only from Ecstasy. We look forward to bringing you many more books from your favorite authors and also the very finest work from new authors of contemporary romantic fiction.

As always, we are striving to present the unique, absorbing love stories that you enjoy most—books that are more than ordinary romance. Your suggestions and comments are always welcome. Please write to us at the address below.

Sincerely,

The Editors
Candlelight Romances
1 Dag Hammarskjold Plaza
New York, New York 10017

It wasn't the hardest thing he'd ever done—not compared with, say, riding a destroyer through sixty-foot seas or walking a girder high enough off the ground to kiss a Cessna. And the fact that the second thing was part of the equation at all was the reason he was standing here, outside the clinic, shuffling like an adolescent with a corsage.

He had to go in. He'd come this far. One five-month series had already begun and ended without him because he couldn't muster the guts to do more than make an inquiring call. A New Year's resolution down the hopper, and here was Tom Pagano, in April, still slogging to work every day with new excuses for staying on the ground.

He swallowed, grabbed the door handle, let it go. Did he want this help or not? A Jack Daniel's or three after a lousy day, that was all the help he'd ever needed.

A tall man with a mustache was coming up the walk to the entrance. Tom made a show of checking his watch and glancing around, as though waiting for someone. He watched the guy go in and wondered if he was part of this phobia group too.

11

He felt a little better. He'd pictured it all women, small old-maidish men . . . and him.

He checked his watch again, for real this time. Ten to five. He was definitely going in now. Definitely. Now.

He opened the door. The receptionist looked up with a benevolent, robotlike smile and asked whether she could help him.

"The phobia workshop," he said too loudly.

"Yes?"

She was going to make him spell it out. He ground his teeth. "I'm here for that. Which room?"

The vacant cheer never faltered. "Down the hall. First door on your right." He thanked her tightly and went where she'd pointed. He had no idea what he'd find. All he knew was that he'd committed himself to meet with a bunch of people weekly for five months—average everyday types, like him, who wanted to get rid of some quirky fear.

He entered a waiting room with another room opening off it. Six or eight faces checked him out and then gazed carefully elsewhere. His heart sank to his Pumas. All women, and one balding man in a wrinkled suit.

He stood for a minute. Every muscle said, Move, Pagano, turn around and shag yourself out of here —this tea party's not for you.

But behind him a real voice said, "Excuse me . . . ?" He turned and there were three more coming in, and he was trapped.

Sarah surveyed the new group while Viv, the psychologist who was the leader, gave her welcoming talk. As usual Sarah tried to match up what she remembered of the participants' fact sheets with the faces. The other aides were doing the same thing and trying, as she was, not to be obvious about it. Scattered around the room were several pairs of eyes darting from side to side, but the heads never moved.

She'd only be working with one person this time, an acrophobic. He could be any of the three men in the group. The short man with the reddish fringe looked likable. Maybe he was the one. She tried to remember the file. Her man was thirty-nine and divorced. What did he do? Was he a printer? No, the printer was the Oriental. Oh, a builder. That was it. He owned a construction firm. She recalled thinking how ironic that was, a builder who had trouble with heights. The poor guy must be having a rough time.

It had to be the dark-haired one in the aviator glasses with the strong cleft chin. Sarah watched him from the corners of her eyes, her attention seemingly on Viv. What an attractive man! He was as muscular as a professional athlete, but a large, full lower lip made him sensuous-looking. There was strength in his face and his body language; this was a guy who'd take no nonsense from anyone.

You could tell he was used to doing things his way. That must be why he looked so out of place in here. He was scowling and fidgeting, and Sarah was full of sympathy. She could remember very clearly what it was like to sit in this group for the first time, feeling like a mutant.

By sheer luck the seat he'd taken turned out to be nearly at the end of the circle, so Tom could hear most of the others introduce themselves before he had to.

After they'd all filed into this big conference room he'd been busy looking around, and he'd missed half of what the leader said . . . but it didn't matter. That was what opening talks were for—so everyone could check things out and settle in. He'd given plenty of them himself, at meetings with clients. He didn't expect anyone to listen. He could recite a shopping list in pig Latin and they'd nod attentively.

But he was listening carefully to the thirteen group members and the aides as each spoke for a couple of minutes. So far things were looking okay. There were more men than he'd expected. He himself seemed to be a mild case. All the aides, he discovered, were people who'd been cured of their own phobias in the program.

He wondered which aide would turn out to be "his," which would work alone with him in weekly practice sessions as he got used to heights again. Probably the detective or the trucker. In fact, the detective was the one who'd passed him outside. Interesting to think that these guys had once had fears too.

It was almost his turn. The woman next to him was talking. Earlier, in a few quick glances, he'd pegged her as someone in his category—a per-

14

fectly normal person with some little quirk. She was in her forties, neat, capable-looking, but he listened with growing wonder as she related a string of her personal horrors, from elevators to shopping malls to snakes, for crying out loud. If it existed, she was afraid of it. Discouragement gnawed at him again. With people like this needing so much help, the meeting time would get all used up every week. He might never—

"Tom?"

The leader was looking at him expectantly. So was everyone else.

"I, uh . . ." He cleared his throat, annoyed at how nervous he'd gotten all of a sudden. What was the big deal? He'd spoken in bigger groups than this plenty of times.

"I'm Tom Pagano," he began again in a much stronger voice. "I'm in construction. And I'm, ah, having a little trouble with heights that I'd like to get cleared up."

The leader nodded encouragingly. Her face was a bland and happy mask. Did she come from the same manufacturer as the receptionist?

"That's it," he said.

The face lost a touch of its jollity and went on to the next patient. She, too, had a closet full of fears; he listened as they tumbled out. Well, he sure was about the most normal person in this bunch. Fat lot of time he was likely to get in the meetings. He'd just have to hope the practice sessions would do the trick. That made more sense than all this talking, anyway. A focused approach. If one of these guys was going to be working along with him in the actual buildings while he got this damn thing knocked, that ought to be enough. He could live with putting in his time at the meetings for five months.

Sarah yawned. It was so stuffy. She tried to shake off her drowsiness and pay attention. Everyone had spoken, and Viv was announcing the aide assignments. She really ought to listen.

"Peg and Marjorie will work with Patrick," Viv said, reading from papers in her lap. "Joan is with Emily. Anne, Martha, and Kim work with Carol." As Viv spoke the aides nodded and smiled at their assignees. "Tom works with Sarah. Walter and Mary go with Bob . . ."

Sarah turned to Tom, but her friendly grin slowly wilted as she saw his face. She thought he must have something bothersome on his mind; that thunderhead of a scowl couldn't have anything to do with her. But he was looking straight in her direction. . . .

Viv ended with instructions for everyone to see their aides and schedule work sessions. Sarah got her things together and picked up her coat. But when she looked around for Tom, he was gone.

"I understand how you must be feeling," Viv said soothingly, "but I'm sure you'll find—"

"Never mind how I'm feeling. I know a dumb decision when I see one." Tom tried to keep his voice down. The waiting room was hardly private, and he didn't care to create a sideshow. He'd simply asked the woman to step away from the others

16

for a minute so they could straighten out this mistake, and that was all he wanted to do. Now it seemed it wasn't a mistake.

"Do you mean to tell me," he demanded, "that you people actually put some *thought* into assigning that girl to me? When there are two male aides who, any fool can see, would be much more—"

"Tom, my sense is that you're overreact—"

"Appropriate for my situation? I need to go up on buildings. Buildings! We're not talking shopping malls here. What the hell kind of use can that little girl be to me?"

The group leader's long thin face was set in doggedly patient lines. "I'll ignore your calling Sarah a little girl, Tom, and just—"

"Don't ignore it. It's the whole point. That wasn't a put-down. She's a small female person. Someone that size would do me as much good on a roof as a Barbie doll."

Vivian forced a smile. "I know how hard this is for you, but you'll be amazed at how soon you'll be sharing thoughts instead of denying. And, Tom, you can take my word for this: Whether your aide is a man or a woman, tall or short, makes no difference."

Tom pushed back his thick brown hair. He felt almost helpless against the shrinky-dink claptrap pouring from the woman's mouth—a very uncharacteristic sensation. He didn't want to lose his temper—he'd sworn to see the workshop through, no matter what—but he had to get this settled.

He said, "I'll explain one more time. I came here

17

to take care of a problem. I'm paying for competent, professional help. You have two guys to pick from who'd be fine. But you're trying to fob me off with some twit who could be a kindergarten teacher." Viv looked strange, as if she might be feeling sick or something, but he pushed on. "I don't like giving you a hard time, but I want this fixed. Let the girl go hold someone's hand in Woolworth's, and reassign one of the men to me. Then there'll be no problem."

Viv was looking at a point behind his left shoulder. He turned. The twit was there.

Standing up, she wasn't as small as he'd thought, and she had a shape that opened the field of suitable occupations beyond kindergarten teacher. But he could see that she'd heard that crack and more. The pointy-chinned face was trying to stay cool.

"Nothing personal," he told her. "I'm trying to solve something here."

"No problem," she said, surprising him. Her expression had gone rigidly businesslike. Well, too bad she'd happened to hear him state the matter so honestly, but at least she was being square about it.

"Sarah," Viv said, putting a hand on each one's shoulder, "Tom was telling me he saw the potential for a teeny conflict here. But I know if you two just take a minute to back-and-forth with it, you can nip this in the bud. Hm?" She looked from one to the other, her smile radiating unshakable faith in the miracle of communication.

Sarah and Tom's eyes met for the briefest instant as they both fought the urge to reiterate the "potential for a teeny conflict" in more accurate words. But the moment of commonality was quickly gone as Sarah marshaled her training to try to get this assignment off on the right foot. The man's remarks had stung, but she needed to remember that she wasn't the one wrestling with an embarrassing problem, ready to vent her tension on any handy target.

Viv gripped their shoulders. "I'll leave you to it, then. And, Tom—you're going to make it. I know you are."

Sarah watched his eyes track Viv as she left, his face a study in what-have-I-gotten-myself-into.

"Is she always like that?" he asked.

Sarah bit off her diplomatic "Like what?" and said instead, "Yes." Why be obtuse? They had enough trouble getting through to each other already. And they hadn't even tried it yet. "Now," she said, "we have to set a time for your first work session. Let's go over here."

She sat in a molded plastic chair that might once have been turquoise and took out her appointment book. Her forehead was damp, and she pushed her sandy brown hair behind her ears and away from her brow, but the shaggy bangs fell right over her face again. She turned. Tom wasn't in the chair next to her. She looked up. He was still standing. "Sit," she coaxed.

"No."

She gave him a disgusted glance and stood. She'd play this charade out like a pro if it killed her. "All right. We'll talk this way. What days are good for you?"

"You don't understand," he said. "This isn't going to work."

Several retorts sprang to Sarah's mind. She resisted them. "What," she asked through teeth that could have been cemented together, "isn't going to work?" One thing that wasn't, as far as she was concerned, was carrying on this conversation standing up. She felt dwarfed. That could get intimidating if she let it. He didn't tower over her; he was just *large*. He kind of *loomed* there, big all over. Everything about him seemed a size larger than normal. Even his glasses. The aviator lenses glinted in the fluorescent light like Jeep headlamps.

"This arrangement," he said. "I guess you couldn't help overhearing what I told that quack—"

"You mean the group leader," Sarah said. "Sure, I could have helped it. I could have walked away. But as long as I didn't," she went on, her wide brown eyes trying to penetrate the smoky glass that partly hid his blue ones, "we might as well clear the air. Exacty what bothers you about my being your aide?"

She thought she saw a tinge of reluctant respect in the barely upturned corners of his mouth. "Do you want me to be honest?"

She sighed. "Usually when someone asks that, they're looking for an excuse to unload some rotten things they can get away with by saying, 'Well, you told me to be honest.'"

The corners turned up a hair more. "Is that what you expect me to do?"

"I don't know what to expect. I've never met you before," Sarah said. She'd about had it with the verbal rugby match. "You could juggle can openers while whistling 'Skip to My Lou,' and it wouldn't surprise me, because I wouldn't know you don't ordinarily do that."

The half smile was gone. "I don't have to listen to this."

"No," Sarah said sweetly, "you don't."

He started to leave. Sarah wanted nothing more than to let him, but a mental picture of one of Vivian's lectures, full of lead-footed earnestness and phony understanding, made her call, "Wait." When he turned, she said, "All right. Your point. Let's backtrack. You don't want me as your aide?"

He glared at her for a minute. "That's right. I want one of the male aides. I have nothing against you personally. Or I didn't, until you showed your teeth."

She did her best to ignore that. She also ignored the impulse to show them again. "Why do you want a man?"

He turned away and jammed his hands in his pockets. "Do you know what the hell I'm here for?"

"Certainly I know. We're all familiar—"

"Then it should be obvious why. It makes no sense that I didn't get one of the men in the first place. I'm a guy, last time I looked. I have trouble with heights. Buildings, roofs. I need someone to help me out with that."

21

Sarah said quietly, "So?"

"*So*, how can a person your size handle it?"

"Will you please," she said, letting her composure slip for the first time, "stop harping on my size as if I were a chihuahua? I'm five-three and I weigh a hundred and fifteen pounds. I won't waft away like a Kleenex on the first strong breeze. Besides, I could be a midget and still function just fine as your aide." Her tone was getting too loud and defensive. "Look," she went on in a softer voice, "whatever you think will happen to you on a roof . . . it won't. Are you afraid you'll fall down, pass out, yell?"

"Something like that," he mumbled. "All I know is, it makes a lot more sense to have someone there who—"

"Every phobic person is afraid of that. But it never happens. You don't need a male aide to cope with those things, because they aren't going to occur." She sat in the plastic chair.

Now he sat too. "Well, as you couldn't wait to point out before, who are you to say what I'm going to do?"

"On the whole, nobody. I know how phobics behave, but I'm not a therapist, if that's what you mean. None of the aides are. We all have other jobs, and we're specially trained in this work. Women *and* men," she couldn't help adding.

"How long have you been doing this?"

"A year."

"A *year?*"

"*Yes*, a year."

"Give me a break," he said. "It takes longer than

that to learn bricklaying. I was led to believe that I was getting an experienced person."

"You got one. But why you're making such a big deal about this is beyond me," Sarah said, "since you made it extremely plain in group that you're fixing to clear up this little problem in a flash. Hey, don't hassle me. I just came for the refreshments." Bite on *that*, you overbearing, obnoxious—

"How old are you?" he asked abruptly.

She glared. "Twenty-eight. Not that it's any of—"

"You look about twenty-two."

"And *you* look determined to make this whole process as hard as possible!" With an effort she dropped her voice. "You know, you remind me of Tiger Lily, my cat. If you catch her at something that makes her look silly, she just pretends it didn't happen. Here you are, pinning me to the wall with your insistence on competent help while trying to convince everyone you don't need any. Then I point that out, and you just attack from another direction. I'm trying to be patient, but you keep fighting me."

He took off his glasses. His eyes were a darker blue than she'd thought, with little creases at the corners, as though he laughed a lot. Sarah told herself not to hold her breath while waiting to see that proven.

"Don't take it so personally," he said. "I'm not fighting you; I'm fighting a poor piece of management. Of course, you probably see it as yelling at the umpire."

"Not at all. Yelling at the umpire is polite."

A maintenance man ambled into the waiting room, pushing a standing pail whose smell made Sarah's eyes sting. She got up, sniffing.

"We're going outside," Tom told her, and kept a guiding hand lightly at her back as they left the clinic. Whether it was that gesture or just her sense reasserting itself, Sarah didn't know, but she decided to try one final time to solve this. He'd managed to pull her into a tug-of-war, and they were getting nowhere. She'd have to make some sort of concession, though she'd rather drink turpentine.

"Look, Tom," she said as they came out into twilit Barkham Street, "the program is the only one in Boston, and it's really good. I've seen it help tons of people in the course of my minuscule experience." She smiled and was rewarded with the shadow of a half grin.

"Sometimes the aide assignments don't work out," she went on. "There can be a personality clash. We're not supposed to say this so early in the program, but if you've been working with your aide for a time and you think it's a bad match, you can get a change."

They turned left on Beacon. "Then why not just save time and do it now?"

"It doesn't work that way. Besides, even if you request a new aide later, you won't get one of the men. There are only Bob and Patrick, and they've been aides a long time. They're always assigned to the more complex cases."

He stopped walking. "Why didn't you or Dr.

24

Get-in-Touch-With-Your-Feelings explain that before?"

"Oh, honestly! Would it have made any difference? As it was, you were acting as if my experience could fit in a bug's eye."

"What did I do with my keys?" he mumbled, patting his jacket pockets.

Sarah had to laugh. "Meow," she said. He looked startled for a second, and then she saw where the lines by his eyes had come from. The corners of his mouth rose in a wide grin that made his face completely different. The glower that had looked as though it could only be removed surgically was gone.

"Well?" Sarah pressed. "Can we make an appointment?"

He took out his wallet. "Here's my card. Call me."

With every fiber she wanted to say, "Here's mine—call *me.*" But it was her appeasement that had made the only dent in his stubbornness. Why risk a turnaround for a moment of satisfaction? She pocketed the card. He unlocked the brown Pontiac they were standing next to and got in.

She looked around. For heaven's sake! Her car was two blocks up Beacon; she should have turned right when they came out of Barkham. Tom had such an attitude that she'd just mindlessly followed him.

Tom drove off, and Sarah turned and headed up the street, muttering.

CHAPTER TWO

"A Mr. Pagano on three, returning your call, Sarah. Bedroom voice."

"Barnyard personality. Thanks, Linda." She pushed the lit button. "Tom?"

"ProTemp? Isn't that an employment agency?" he asked without preamble.

"Yes," she said.

"You work in an employment agency?"

Sarah took a deep breath, held it, let it out. It didn't help. "That's right. I also read the comics and Ann Landers before the front page. I'm a college dropout. If a documentary comes on, I change the channel. There—now you won't have to keep looking for proof of how unqualified I am to be your phobia aide. I just gave you all of it. No, wait—sometimes I leave clinic staff meetings early so I won't miss *Barney Miller*."

There was silence. She could hear him breathing. She covered her eyes. Ugh. She'd let him put her on the defensive with two sentences. Had she been taking cretin lessons?

"Relax," he said.

She tried to do just that. She shouldn't have

given in to the luxury of being sarcastic. The trouble was, the two days she'd let pass before phoning him had, instead of serving to let tempers cool, just built tension. She was so defensive that she'd jumped ten feet.

"Well," she said, "thanks for returning my call. I'd like to set an appointment for a work session."

"Meow," he said.

Sarah laughed. Maybe she'd survive this assignment. "After work today or tomorrow is good for me. Around six?"

"Tomorrow I have plans. Today is okay. Where?"

"Meet me in front of the clinic and we'll go from there."

"Go where?"

Sarah rubbed her eyes again. "I don't know yet. I need to hear more about your phobia first. Then we'll decide on a starting point."

"*We'll* decide? Or *you* will?"

"We. Will."

"Right."

While she steeled herself to deal with whatever he was going to say next, he hung up.

Sarah parked on Beacon at five past six and hurried around the corner to the clinic. She hated to be late, especially for a first work session, but Copley Square traffic had been a blaring tangle.

It wasn't raining yet, but the sky was dark. The air held a cold sting, more like February than April. She pulled up her raincoat hood to warm her ears. Her watch said six-ten. Maybe she ought to walk around and look for the Pontiac. He might be waiting in it. Since there was no parking or standing on Barkham, he'd have to be on a nearby block.

But if she left to look, she wouldn't be here if he did come.

She rubbed her hands together, then stuck them in her pockets. Her gloves were in her wool coat, which was in her closet at home. This had been one of those two-faced days, so sweet and sunny in the morning that you couldn't believe it would turn so raw.

Six-twenty. The wind was getting snappy, and a few drops were starting to fall. Sarah's hood blew off for the third time; she pulled the drawstring to close it around her head and tied it. Only her shaggy bangs showed. She knew that with her large brown eyes this made her look like an inquisitive ant, but she was too cold to care.

Tom's Pontiac pulled up, and she ran over and got in. She hadn't realized on Tuesday that he had a scent, a very distinctive one. But the impression came back to her now as the car's aroma settled over her, a smell of warm skin and faintly minty breath.

She pushed back her hood and shook her head to fluff the plastered-down hair. Drops flew from her bangs, and Tom winced.

"You got me in the eye," he said. "And that coat is wetting my upholstery. Take it off. I'll put it on the floor in back."

Immediately Sarah was embarrassed—and angry. She was barely in the car, and he was already telling her what to do in his usual dictatorial way.

"Maybe," she said, "you'd rather I just rode in the trunk."

"Hell, no. That'd never dry."

She couldn't seem to let go of this. "You'd also have a dead body to deal with sooner or later."

"At least those don't talk."

She squeezed her palms together in an effort to simmer down. She wished his neck was between them.

"I will not take my coat off," she said. "I'm sorry if I'm getting the car wet"—she was as sorry as if she'd won a trip to Europe—"but it'll dry, and it's your fault, anyway, for being late. I wouldn't be cold and rained on if you'd been on time."

"I was on time. You weren't."

She looked sharply at him. "You were here at six?"

"Yes."

"I hit traffic. But it was only five after."

He shrugged one shoulder. "Doesn't matter to me. I made a phone call in the meantime. You're the one being picky about the time."

Sarah leaned back into the soft seat and stared straight ahead. He'd gotten her on the defensive again, even faster this time, and she'd cooperated fully. Here, tiger, open your mouth and let me stick my arm in.

She watched the wipers' steady swipes and tried to figure a way to start over. Instead she found herself wondering who he'd called and what plans he had for the following night.

29

"Well," she said crisply. She turned and looked at him. In profile his nose was a little bumpy, his lower lip not quite so generous. She didn't know much about whiskers, but his looked as though he'd last shaved about twelve hours ago. Six A.M. Did he get up that early?

Who *cared?*

"Well," she said again, and realized that while she'd been daydreaming they'd gone several blocks and were now far from her car.

"I generally do this type of session with my own car, but I guess it's silly to turn around," she said. "Let's head over to Huntington Avenue."

"Why?"

"What?"

"Why?"

Don't let him get you jumping up and down and blowing smoke out of your ears again, Sarah. Just answer the question.

"Because there are some buildings there I work with."

"What did you have in mind to do?" he asked, making no move to turn toward Huntington.

Throw you off one of them.

"Well?" he demanded.

Don't take it as a challenge. Just think of him as a man with a toothache who wants to see the needle first.

"We're going to park in front of a building and look at it while we talk," she said. "Then we'll go in and do some exercises."

He must have been satisfied, because he turned left, toward Huntington. He parked where Sarah

30

directed and rested his arm along the back of the seat. But he pulled it away quickly when he touched the wet upholstery.

Sarah resisted the impulse to point out that water didn't corrode skin.

Tom's nerves were starting to bubble a little, and he tried to distract himself by concentrating on what was in front of him. What was in front of him at the moment was a young woman with soft-looking hair that had gotten a little wet. She had good skin and pink cheeks. Maybe it was makeup, but he doubted that. A kind of heat came from her; there was dampness on her forehead and upper lip that wasn't from the rain, and something about her color told him it was related.

This raincoat she was wearing looked like the tarps he had his men hang when they broke through a wall. He bet if he touched it, it would have the same stiff, waxy feel. But he remembered how she looked without it, all nice small curves.

Her face was in motion now as she talked. He watched the feathery lashes move over the big dark eyes. Her upper lip was pointy, her lower one big, like his.

His glasses were getting misty in the closed car, and he took them off and wiped them on his jacket sleeve. When he looked up again, she was staring at him expectantly. He realized he hadn't heard anything she'd said.

"I'm sorry," he told her. "I wasn't listening."

Sarah found herself smiling. An honest confession, however tiny, and an apology, were beams of sunshine from Tom Pagano.

31

"I asked whether elevators bother you."

"No."

"Staircases?"

"No."

"What about looking out a window on a high floor?"

He turned away and stayed silent. The moment stretched on.

She said, "Why don't you paw the ground once for no and twice for yes?"

"Damn it, you—"

"I can't help if you won't let me," Sarah said tightly. The lift she'd felt a minute ago was gone. "I need answers to these questions before we can —oh, never mind." She opened her door. "Let's just go in and play it by ear."

The five-story building had professional offices on the first two floors and apartments above. Tom followed Sarah up one flight. There was a window at the landing and a fire escape.

"Have a look out," Sarah said.

He walked to the window. Looking straight on, there was nothing to be seen but another building past the dark, wet metal of the fire escape.

"Can you look down?" Sarah asked, watching him carefully.

Of course he could. He dropped his eyes. There was where the fire escape ended. There was the wet pavement of the alley, illuminated by a streetlight. He felt the bubble again.

"Are you having levels?" she asked.

He was looking at the bricks on the opposite

wall, gauging how many rows there were between him and the ground. "What?"

"Levels. Remember, from the meeting?"

He did, vaguely. You were supposed to grade how nervous you were on a scale of ten.

"I guess so."

"How much?"

"Oh—give it a two or three."

"Take a good long look, left and right."

He did. He felt funny.

"Still three?"

"Maybe four."

"Okay. Let's go up one more."

He followed her up again. This time she'd removed her coat, and he had something to take his mind off this whole business. Her bottom was round and just mobile enough beneath her gray wool skirt.

He was sorry when they got to the third floor. His brain remembered why they were there, even while his hormones were still climbing a flight of steps behind a curvaceous lady.

Sarah pointed at the window. "Try this one."

He did it the way he had downstairs, looking straight ahead at the brick wall first, then gradually down, then side to side.

"Where's your level now?"

"Two . . . one," he said with surprise. "Nothing much at all."

She smiled. "Good."

He wondered why he was less nervous on the third floor than on the second. He thought of asking Sarah about it. Instead he said, "This is stupid."

Her smile disappeared. "Why do you think so?"

"I just don't see what good it can do. Looking out windows. Saying how I *feel.*" He pronounced the word as though it were one he wouldn't use in front of a church group.

It was getting easier to swim past his bait. Since everything that came out of his mouth ranged from irritating to hateful, she was becoming practiced. If only she had more experience with four-year-olds. . . .

"I'm sorry you don't like talking about how you feel," Sarah said, "but you'd better force yourself, because it helps to do a lot of that. Though with me, at least, you can do it in English. I don't like those phony expressions any more than you do. As for what good it does—let's go down and I'll explain."

Following Sarah down wasn't nearly as nice as walking up behind her had been. Having nothing better to do, Tom listened to what she was saying, more or less.

"The goal, naturally, is to get you out on top of tall buildings. So we do that bit by bit, starting with getting the feel of different heights from inside. You know how the third-floor window was easier than you expected just now? That was because you'd already dealt with the second floor. Okay. You go alone now."

"Where?"

"Up one flight. When you get to the top, tell me."

Was that his punishment for busting her chops? he wondered ridiculously. What would she do after that, string a rope between this building and the next and hand him a parasol?

He'd thought the session was over and had started to relax. Not that the things he'd had to do were so tough; what made him half nuts was the suspense of waiting to see what this Styrofoam-brain would dream up next and worrying about reacting in some embarrassing way.

Sarah watched as he climbed the stairs, absently appreciating the way his rear bulged and then tautened at each step.

"Here," he called.

She told him to look out the window and asked for his levels. She sent him up another flight, went up one more herself, and repeated the exercise. Then she looked at her watch and was thrilled to see that it was seven-thirty.

"That's enough for now," she called up the stairs, and he ran down. He was past her and out of the building before she could close her mouth.

He drove her back to her car. The rain had settled into a steady shower that looked like it would never stop. There wasn't much heat on, and Sarah felt chilled. The warm-skin scent she'd noticed in the car before had been replaced by a wet-animal smell. Probably her coat. Yuck.

She was also tired and very hungry. She started the Buick and made her way to Route 9, her big tires sending up sprays as she went. Should she broil that hunk of scrod or bake it? Broiling was faster. She still had the fat asparagus she'd bought Saturday. Potato? Sure. Or maybe a slice of that Italian bread with the sesame seeds. She'd eaten a frozen low-calorie dinner last night; she could spend some calories. Besides, she needed nourishment. She felt as though she'd done ten miles as part of a dogsled team.

She turned off Route 9 in Newton, just a bit past Chestnut Hill, and pulled into the lot behind her building. Oh, no—the yellow Toyota was there. Not tonight! The office had been a zoo, the work session as close to torture as it was possible to come. She was cold and wet; she wanted dinner, a bath, and TV.

"Grandma?" she said as she unlocked her door.

"Hi, dear." Jan Hellerman dislodged Sarah's fat tiger cat from her lap and went to kiss her. The inconvenienced cat glared. "I guess you saw the car. Good thing I came. Your little piggy was ravenous."

She's not the only one, Sarah thought.

"I could hardly wait for you to come home. You won't believe what I found. You're later than usual, though, aren't you? Have you had dinner?"

"No," Sarah said passionately, wondering what treasure was in store for her.

"Oh. You must have had a whozit."

"Work session."

"What is it this time? Buses, bridges . . . ?"

"Heights."

"What a shame," her grandmother said. "How can one enjoy a view?"

"One can't. In this man's case he can't run his business too well, either, since he's a builder. Listen, why don't I pour you a drink while I—"

"Oh, no. No, dear. Don't go to trouble. I'll just

give you your present and run. You're going to love this!"

"Don't tell me you found a garage sale on a cloudy Thursday?"

"No. I bought this Sunday, but I've been too busy to get over here."

Couldn't you have been busy just one more night? Sarah thought, and promptly felt awful. She adored her grandmother, and though the one-bedroom apartment couldn't house many more of her precious finds, Sarah supposed she could have a more inconvenient hobby. Writing crank letters. Setting fires.

"Don't turn around till I tell you," the short gray-haired woman said, and Sarah heard paper crackling. Then, "Look now!"

Sarah turned. It was a vase of giant peacock feathers. Her grandmother had set it on the floor by the couch, and the feathers had a frondlike effect that was pretty in that corner. The only trouble was, the dark greenish-blue was deadly next to the brown sofa.

"Lily was *so* curious about the package," Jan said as they watched the cat rise on her hind legs to sniff the feathers. "She must be wondering where the rest of the peacock is."

Sarah laughed and started into the kitchen, but Jan sat down and patted the sofa cushion.

"So? What do you think?"

"They're beautiful," Sarah said, guilty that she had to be prompted. It must be her hunger; after just coffee for breakfast and a yogurt lunch interrupted by an applicant, it was interfering with her

37

response mechanism. "Thank you. Lily and I will enjoy them."

Jan looked at her watch. "I'll be running in a minute. There's a comedy special on cable with that darling boy."

"What darling boy?"

"You know. Whatzis. Eddie Murphy."

Sarah gaped. "Eddie Murphy? Isn't he a little . . . racy?"

"Not for me, dear. Let's hear about this builder of yours. Are you going to have to scale high-rises with him?"

"Ha. I'll be happy just to have a polite conversation."

"Oh? Is he rude?"

"Terribly. He argues with everything I say."

"Then," her grandmother said, "maybe you ought to say less."

That thought came back to Sarah near midnight as she fished some Tums from her night-table drawer and turned off the lamp. Her stomach was noisy; she'd finally had dinner at ten o'clock and had eaten too fast. Sometimes her grandmother said cryptic things that turned out to be smart once you pondered them. Was this one of those times?

No, she decided, closing her eyes. What she said or didn't say to Tom Pagano made no difference. He had a problem with his problem—but she didn't. Her only problem was his real problem.

Unravel *that*, Grandma.

CHAPTER THREE

Sarah made sure to be early this time. If they were going to have another bad start, it wouldn't be because she didn't bend over sideways to avoid it.

Tom was ten minutes late. She ignored it. She was going to ignore everything less hostile than a shotgun.

She noticed his scent again as she got into his car. She still would have preferred to take hers—she felt more in control of the session that way—but it seemed important to him that they go in his. Probably for the same reason.

"What am I supposed to do today?" Tom asked her.

"We're going to . . ." She couldn't get her seat belt fastened. She'd pulled it as far as it would go, but it didn't reach the clasp. "We're . . ."

"I'll do that." They'd come to a red light. He pulled the handbrake and reached across Sarah to give the belt a good yank. She looked at his hands as he slipped the metal tab into the buckle. They were wide and rough-looking with fingers that moved quickly and confidently. Warmth melted through her as her mind suddenly filled with notions of what those hands might do to a woman's body. How would the fingers feel, stroking the skin of secret places?

She looked a little further. He was wearing a short-sleeved shirt and his arms had a lot of dark straight hair. It took real effort for Sarah to stop herself from touching it; she wanted to know whether it was coarse or soft and how the sun-browned skin felt. She leaned forward to see whether the same type of hair showed by his collar. The belt tightened, reminding her that she was being a fool, and she sat back. *There is no room here*, she told herself sternly, *for this kind of certifiable behavior. I will cut it out immediately, as of this instant.*

"Well?" he said.

"Uh"—she wiped her brow with shaky fingers—"we're going to Clarendon Street, to a building like last week's. We'll do a little more than before."

"Why don't we just go back to the same place?"

"Because you've been there. It's too familiar."

"Right," he said with just a hint of reluctance. Maybe the weather had put him in a good mood. The sun, finally out after days of rain, had warmed the air to an un-April-like seventy-eight degrees. Everybody she met seemed happy today.

"I'd like you to look out windows some more. Maybe from a higher floor. And we'll try a little outside work if you feel ready."

His expression didn't change, but she saw him swallow. "Outside?"

"Not a roof yet. A low fire escape. I know you'll do just fine."

40

Her quiet, patient tone reminded him of his first impression of her as a kindergarten teacher, and he chuckled.

Sarah clenched her fists. She'd sworn to stay cool, but they hadn't been together for ten minutes and he was laughing at her already. She wished she could dangle him down an elevator shaft.

"There's nothing funny," she said. "You don't have to shout amen to everything I say, but at least have the common courtesy—"

"Hold it, hold it." Tom glanced behind him, changed lanes, and slowed.

"What are you doing? We're going to Clarendon—"

"I said, *hold it.*" He stopped at the curb. "We have a little misunderstanding here." He rested his arm along the seat back and leaned toward Sarah. He took off his glasses and looked straight at her. "Something popped into my mind that made me laugh. It had nothing to do with . . . well, with what you were talking about. I happened to laugh at a bad moment, and I'm sorry." He pulled back into traffic.

Sarah sat, dumbfounded. Those were the most words she'd heard in one clip from Tom Pagano; mostly he acted as though someone had once told him he was the strong, silent type and he'd decided to make a career of it. Plus, he'd shown some sensitivity. *Plus*, he'd apologized. Second time since she'd known him.

And he smelled different today. When he leaned over, she'd caught something . . . after-

41

shave? No. Sweeter. More . . . feminine. As if someone's perfume had stayed on his shirt. Her throat felt strange, and she coughed.

Anyway, what had they been talking about? Going out on a fire escape.

Was that perfume?

What difference did it make?

"Is that—are you—what kind of after-shave do you have on?" Sarah asked, not knowing what was going to come out of her mouth until too late.

She'd turned to the window to hide her embarrassment; she didn't see when he looked her way for such a long moment that he had to brake suddenly for a light.

"I don't," he said.

"Oh. There was something . . . something must . . ." *I wish I had never started this,* Sarah thought. *I wish the session could begin again. I wish I was in Antarctica.* "I smelled something, and I asked because—because it's like a perfume I use." Don't stop now, Sarah. You're just warming up. A few more minutes of this marvelously creative improvisation and you won't have a session to worry about at all. The man won't want to be on the same block with you, never mind a fire escape.

"It must be your own, then."

"No. I'm not wearing it today." She tried to come up with something else to talk about, but she couldn't think what year it was, much less change the subject.

"It can stay on your clothes," he said.

Right.

42

"Oh. I know what you—uh . . ." His voice trailed off.

"Yes?"

"Nothing."

Sarah felt awful. Had he figured out that she was having those crazy thoughts about him? Maybe that was why he looked so squirmy. But maybe it had nothing to do with that.

She had to know what he'd started to say. "I wish you'd continue."

"Oh, hell. I guess it doesn't matter. I figured out what you smell, that's all. My sunblock."

She felt a ridiculous current of relief. Ridiculous because she was happy that the smell wasn't a woman's perfume. What *was* going on?

He was still talking, explaining how his nose got reindeer-red even in the spring if he stayed outdoors at a construction site. It was clear that he didn't want to admit he used something as wimpy as sunscreen, but she liked that he'd finally said it. Fortunately he didn't wind down until they got to Clarendon Street. By then Sarah was alert and functioning once more. She didn't know why she'd acted like such an airhead. She just wanted to make sure it wouldn't happen again.

"The windows in this one are a little different," she told Tom as they went into the building. "They're bigger, and they look out toward the back instead of the side. So you see a wider field."

Tom was quiet. His man-of-few-words demeanor seemed to have returned.

She stopped by the stairs. "Why don't you go up

to the landing while I stay here? Tell me what you see when you look out."

He went up, and Sarah heard him say something.

"What?" she called.

He spoke again, but she couldn't make out the words. She went up. "I didn't hear you," she said.

"I didn't say much. Just what was out there."

"Well, go on up one more. But talk louder this time."

"No! I don't want the whole building wondering if I'm doing a guided tour in here."

"Nobody's paying any attention. The clinic has an arrangement with the owners—we use the building all the time. Look, just go on up, and then come down and tell me what you saw."

A while later Sarah said, "Feel ready for the fire escape here on the second floor?"

He did the one-shoulder shrug she was getting used to. She was also getting used to what it meant: that he was uneasy about pushing ahead but would choke before he'd admit it.

They opened the window, and Sarah climbed out and sat. Just then she remembered that she'd been so busy kicking that asinine conversation about perfume under the rug that she'd forgotten to discuss tools. It wasn't fair to let him come out without the preparation. Boy, she was skiing without poles today.

"Wait a second," she said as Tom started to get onto the window ledge. "Let's talk about your tools for a minute. What will you use?"

44

He put his foot back down. He looked completely bewildered. "What are you talking about?"

"You know. *Tools.*"

"For what? Is it part of the treatment that I have to get back into the building by breaking in?"

Sarah closed her eyes and prayed for patience.

"What kind of damn tools? I don't walk around with a chainsaw in my back pocket."

"The kind," Sarah said, "that we talk about in group. Often. Often enough that you should be sick of the subject by now, not ignorant of it. The mental exercises you use to distract yourself, so the fear doesn't build. Remember?"

"Vaguely. Playing games in your head with words and numbers, something like that?"

"Right. And touching what's around you, to keep you focused on what's really happening."

"Uh-huh," he said, ostentatiously bored.

"So what will it be? How about one of the number tricks?"

"Okay. I'll count to four hundred by thirty-threes. In Italian."

"Tom—"

"No? How about if I spell all the state capitals south of the Mason–Dixon line backward?"

"For heaven's sake! Will you—" She stopped. "Do you *know* all the capitals south of the Mason–Dixon line?"

He laughed. "Nope. Now, can we get this over with?"

It was as close as he'd come to acknowledging his fear. And he was right—all she was doing now

45

was letting tension mushroom. She nodded and beckoned to him to join her.

Slowly he climbed out onto the slatted metal platform and sat facing Sarah. The sun was setting, and there was a cool breeze, but his forehead was sweaty.

"Use your hands," Sarah reminded him.

He ran them along the metal.

"Tell me what you feel." He frowned, and she chuckled and said, "I mean, literally, what you're touching."

"Oh. Rough spots, chipped paint. My hands are getting flaky with it." He grinned slightly. "Also bird, uh, droppings."

Sarah looked down. "Ugh, you're right. An eagle must have raised a family here. How's your level?"

"Three, four."

"What was it right when you came out?"

"Maybe seven."

"Oh, that high? And you've gotten it down? Good. Let's stand up."

"Eight."

She smiled. "You lowered it before; you'll do it again. Here, I'll go first." She stood. "Now you."

He got up, keeping his eyes straight ahead. Sarah noted that he hadn't looked down yet at all. His forehead was getting wetter.

"You're doing great," she said. "Want to hold my arm?"

He scowled. "No."

"Hold the rail, then. Feel it. What's your level?"

"Eight." He took a hand off the rail to wipe his brow and quickly replaced it.

"How are you going to get your level down?"

"I don't . . ."

"I mean, with what tool? Use a counting exercise. Or concentrate on how you're going to reward yourself when the work session is over."

"With a bourbon. A big one."

"How big?"

His chuckle was strained. "I'll swipe an umbrella stand from one of my buildings."

"How's your level?"

"Four. Hey."

" 'Hey' is right. Now I'm going to be quiet and let you distract yourself."

Sarah looked around, enjoyed the breeze, let her mind wander. It immediately wandered back to what Tom said in the car, after she'd gotten mad at him for laughing. Something about that had been niggling at her; now she had it. He'd said the laugh had nothing to do with what she was talking about, but he'd hesitated, as though he'd been about to say it had nothing to do with her.

That meant it must have had something to do with her.

So he'd been thinking about her. Or laughing about her. Or—

"Hi."

Sarah jumped, and Tom swore. There was a man at the window. A round, blond head was looking up at them.

"Need a hand?" he asked. "I saw the window open. Thought I'd offer some help if you need it."

"That's nice of you," Sarah said, "but we're fine, thanks."

"What did you do, lose something?"

"No. We're—"

"Don't tell him," Tom whispered forcefully without moving his lips.

"Uh . . . actually, yes. We did. We lost a, uh . . . a . . ."

"Cat," Tom said.

"Really? What a shame. Ran away?"

Sarah said, "Yes. Temporarily. I'm sure we'll—"

"I'll help you look. Where did you see him last?"

"Oh, you can't—you don't have to do that."

"Nonsense. What's a neighbor for?" He put a foot on the sill. "I'll just come out, and you can show me where you think the little rascal might have gone."

"That's not—" Sarah had been about to say "necessary," but she no longer needed to say it, since he was on the platform. He wasn't much taller than she was, but the new weight was enough to make the structure shake slightly. She saw Tom close his eyes. Fresh sweat appeared. She had to get the little man back inside as quickly as possible.

"I think he ran in there," she said, pointing to some bushes below. "Why don't you look in that area?"

"Where?" He squeezed between her and Tom on the tiny platform to lean over the rail.

Sarah changed her position to make room for him. As she brushed against Tom he gripped her upper arm and pulled her close. With no warning a weird mix of feelings besieged her. She wanted to smile and cry. The iron-hard thigh pressing

48

against her hip, the strong fingers tight on her arm, were sending hot shocks through her . . . but that was ridiculous, since that wasn't why he was touching her at all!

"Where?" the blond man repeated.

"The tall . . ." She cleared her throat; she sounded hoarse. "The tall bush on the right."

"I'll run down and have a look. Why don't you try up a ways, friend?" he asked Tom. "Just in case he climbed up there. Cats are real daredevils, you know."

He went back through the window, and Sarah felt Tom's body relax a little. He still gripped her arm. She was annoyed at how that made her feel and annoyed with herself for being annoyed.

"We're not going to get rid of him unless we play this out," Sarah whispered.

He was looking better. He let go of her.

"What's the cat's name?" the man shouted from below, and they both jumped again.

Sarah said, "Um, it's . . ."

"Spot," Tom said.

"Here, Spot. Here, kitty." The man pushed between two bushes. "Spot! Come out, come out, wherever you are."

"We'd better join in," Sarah said.

"For God's sake. This is idiotic."

"You started it. Listen, I'm going to climb up. We'll pretend to look for a few minutes, and then we'll leave." She moved toward the stairs.

"Not yet," Tom said, pulling her back. Off-balance, she stepped on her sneaker lace, stumbled, and fell heavily against the rail. The fire escape

49

shimmied and creaked. "God," he breathed. His face went ashy. Sarah could see him struggling with himself, wanting to help her, unable to move.

"I'm fine," she said quickly, though her knee was scraped raw beneath her pants. "What's your level?"

"Nine."

"Not ten? Good."

"Spot! Here, Spot! Here, kitty!"

Still pale, Tom started to laugh softly.

"What's funny?"

He laughed harder.

And then she started, too, because, of course, it was insane, all of it, so insane that it was hilarious. She sank to the platform, unable to stop. Tom was holding his stomach. Tears ran down her face.

"Yo!"

Sarah looked down. She tried to pull herself together. The blond man seemed surprised that they could be so merry when they'd lost their pet. He said, "Any luck?"

"No," she said. "Actually I haven't climbed up yet. I'll do that now." She started up the steps.

"Don't you go, miss. Let the gentleman do it. Those steps are pretty rickety."

She started to laugh again and clamped her hand over her mouth. When she thought she could risk speaking, she said, "I'll go. My friend has a—a bad ankle."

Behind her, Tom coughed.

"Spot!" she called, climbing the narrow stairs. "Where are you?" She went through the motions of looking around, then came down. Tom held the rail but with only one hand. He was trying to keep a straight face.

"Find him?" he asked.

"Smarty Pants. I'm doing all this for you. I should get a Nobel."

Below, the blond man shouted, "Got 'im!"

The claws kneading Sarah's thigh through her jeans were so tiny that she barely felt them.

"You have to admit, he's adorable," she said.

Tom stopped for the light at Trenton Street. "Is he a he?"

"I don't know. I can't tell when they're so little."

He reached over and lifted the stubby orange tail. "Male."

"You're kidding. How do you know?"

"My family had cats."

"He's so tiny. Is he more than a month old, do you think?"

He glanced at the kitten. "Six weeks, maybe. I still don't understand why you told that guy he was yours."

"What choice did I have? He would have gone on looking for our imaginary cat forever."

"Well, you should have waited until the guy was gone and let the cat loose."

"Oh, should I? Look at him, Tom."

He kept his eyes on the road.

"The poor thing would never last outside. You can tell he's a stray; house cats don't get this bedraggled."

He lifted his shoulder. "Doesn't matter to me.

51

You're the one who's going to be crowded. Don't you already have a cat?"

"Yes. And she hates other animals. This whole business is your fault, anyway. I wasn't going to tell that man the truth when he first stuck his head out, but I would have given some more plausible story if you hadn't rattled me. You'll have to take him."

He braked hard. "What?"

"Watch it. He almost fell."

"I can't take a damn cat."

"Why not?"

"I just can't, that's all."

"Where is it you live? Swampscott?"

"Salem."

"Your landlord doesn't allow pets?"

He muttered something.

"Pardon?"

"I, uh—I'm the landlord. Well, they're condos, really, but I built the complex."

"Then it's set." She lifted the kitten and kissed its nose. "You're going to join the Yuppies in Salem, Spot."

"Can it, Sarah. I am not taking this cat."

"We'll bring him to the pound, then."

Tom was quiet for a while. Then, "Do they destroy animals after a month or whatever?"

"I guess so."

Abruptly he changed the subject. "That was some scene on the fire escape."

"Well, you got through it. What do you think about it now? Now that it's over, I mean."

He considered. "I don't know why, but I'm

more optimistic. Isn't that crazy? You'd think I'd be more nervous."

"Not necessarily."

"Why not?"

"You're finding out that your fear won't kill you. Most phobics are afraid they'll choke or have a heart attack. It's easy to believe that's happening when your heart pounds and you get short of breath. But yours got as high as it can and you're fine."

"That wasn't as high as it could get. It was a nine."

She looked at him shrewdly. "Have you ever had a ten?"

He thought. "I'm not sure. I guess not."

"Then that probably *was* a ten."

"Huh?"

"It's all in how you see it. Some people say they have a lot of tens. Others have none. Usually that means they're reserving the number for some horrible feeling they won't ever have. See? You probably just think you've never been as afraid as you can be."

He thought about that while he drove. They were only about half a mile from her car; she'd be getting out soon.

He watched out of the corner of his eye as the kitten climbed Sarah's blouse and settled on her shoulder. She flinched a little as it clawed its way up, but she let it.

He remembered the silky feel of her blouse when he grabbed onto her on the fire escape. And more: her skin, silkier still. Even through his fear he'd been aware of the softness of her arm in his grip. He'd been afraid of hurting her. He'd felt terrible when she tripped and banged against the rail and he couldn't help her.

It wasn't only her arm that was soft, either. There was a moment, a few short seconds that burned now in his memory, when her body had been close against his. He'd felt her, all warm, pillowy curves, next to him from leg to chest. Her hair had touched his lips. He remembered how impossibly sweet it smelled and tasted. He wanted to smell and taste it again.

He pulled up near her Buick. He hadn't paid much attention to it, but it was a beautiful thing—gleaming white with a red plush interior.

"That's some car," he said.

"Isn't it? I love it. It's a Somerset. They only started making them this year."

"It must have a lot of gadgets."

"You bet. It does everything but make my breakfast."

"I wouldn't have, uh—you don't seem like the glitzy car type." Good one, Pagano. Why don't you just call her a dishrag? "I mean, not that you—"

"I know what you mean." She smiled. A dimple appeared in her left cheek. He wondered why he hadn't noticed it before. "Actually you're right. This is the first new car I've ever had. I can't explain why I got it." She shrugged. "I just wanted it."

He understood that, all right.

She said, "So . . ."

He looked away from her, out the windshield.

"You must know somebody you can give this cat to."

"I don't. Not a soul."

"Who takes care of yours if you're not home?"

"My grandmother."

"She lives with you?"

"No. She lives alone, in Brookline."

"Fine, then. How about her?"

"I've tried to give her pets before. She says she's too old."

"How old is she?"

"Seventy-six. She lies about it, but that's her real age."

"Good for her. I sure would."

"Not her way, you wouldn't. She says she's eighty."

He frowned. "What?"

"She thinks—oh, never mind. I'm too tired to explain it."

He gave her another puzzled look and turned away again. "What will we do with him, then? You don't know *anyone?*"

"No. Do you?"

"No." He turned back to her. "I guess I'm it."

She grinned. The brown eyes were huge, warm. "You'll take him?"

"Guess I'll have to."

Sarah detached the kitten from her shoulder, where it had been snoozing noisily, and put it on the seat next to Tom. "Say hi to your sugar daddy, kiddo," she said, stroking it with one finger.

55

Keys buzzed and clicked in Tom's brain. "Would you really have let him go to the pound?"

Sarah simply gazed at him.

"Out," he said, trying hard to look furious.

CHAPTER FOUR

Tom reached into the cabinet for a glass and touched fur. He peered in. Spot lay there, sleeping comfortably between two beer mugs.

He took the kitten out and put him on the floor. He was getting bigger; they grew so fast.

He poured bourbon over ice in the glass and went to the freezer. Since he'd gotten a microwave, frozen dinners had taken on new significance in his life: they were actually edible. Sometimes he even looked forward to them.

But not tonight, he decided, putting back the Salisbury steak and turkey dinners he'd been considering. Tonight he felt like seeing Sarah.

He dialed her number. He'd make her say yes this time. In the three weeks since that fire-escape business had left him seeing her in a different light, he'd been trying to get her to do something other than climb steps with him, but she always refused.

It wasn't that he was crazy about her or anything. She could still be a pain, calling the shots in her schoolteacherish way. It was just that, until that day, he hadn't known she could be fun too. He still found himself smiling whenever he remembered how they'd laughed when that nosy guy had butted in and the whole thing had turned into a Disney movie.

"Hello?"

"Sarah? Tom."

"Tom! I'm glad you called."

"Good. We're going to—"

"You know what's coming up, don't you?"

"Yup. Dinner. You and me, tonight."

There was a small silence. "I meant your building in Allston. We're going up on the roof this week, remember?"

"Sure, I remember. But the reason I called is, I'm taking you to dinner tonight."

"I've already had dinner," Sarah said, eyeing the chicken she'd been about to bake when the phone rang. She opened the hot oven now and put it in. She closed the door with a determined shove. Just in case she was tempted to change her mind.

"Later, then," he said. "We'll go for a ride and get some ice cream."

"Tom—"

"Don't keep fighting me, Sarah."

"That's not . . . what I'm here for."

"It's not what anybody's anywhere for. It just happens. I like you, you like me—"

"I'm your aide."

He took a big swallow of bourbon to keep his mouth busy. He was burning to let her have a few well-chosen words about the aide stuff, but he resisted. No way to make friends.

"Anyway," she said more softly, "it was nice of

you to ask. What day is good for us to go to Allston?"

That aide talk was like a cold shower. He gave up. "Tomorrow after the meeting, I guess."

"Fine."

He hung up and went back to the freezer.

Sarah turned down the visor to block the late-afternoon sun that filled the Pontiac.

"The warm weather looks like it's here to stay," she said.

"Don't be ridiculous," Tom answered. "You know this town. We could have a blizzard tomorrow."

"Shh. Don't tempt fate."

"That isn't the kind of temptation I've been thinking about."

She kept quiet. She was glad she hadn't said yes to any of his invitations. Not that Tom was easy to resist—oh, no. That couldn't be harder if he had had chocolate frosting. He was so different when they were talking about things that had nothing to do with the workshop; naturally she'd be drawn to his nice side and want to see more of it. It was so hard to keep reminding herself that she was doing him the most good for now by being his aide and nothing more.

Tom parked in front of an attractive buff-colored stone building on Weyland Avenue. It had white shutters and window boxes of freshly planted blue petunias.

"How pretty," Sarah said. "When did you build it?"

"Two years ago. I like it too. It's one of my favorites."

"Then you must be twice as upset that it gives you trouble."

He scowled but didn't answer. They climbed the five flights, Tom in the lead. He didn't look toward the windows they passed at each landing. Finally they reached the short metal staircase that led to the roof. Tom hesitated at the bottom.

"Okay?" she asked.

"I'm not sure."

"What's bothering you?"

"Thinking about going out there."

"Think about something else."

"Like what?"

"Something nice."

He began to grin. Quickly she said, "Think about your favorite dessert."

"Dessert after what?" He climbed the stairs.

What the heck. At least the topic was getting him up the steps. "After whatever you like."

Smiling widely now, he pushed down the bar of the heavy door at the top, and they stepped out. The door closed by itself with a decisive *thwump*. His smile started to falter. He looked at the door, then out toward the roof line, then back. He took hold of the doorknob.

"Stay," Sarah coaxed. "Don't go back."

"I wasn't going to."

"Why are you holding the knob?"

"I, uh . . . would you believe I collect them?"

She laughed. "You still haven't told me what your favorite dessert is."

"Let's go back downstairs and I'll tell you anything you want. The history of the pencil. The immediate causes of the Franco-Prussian War."

"No deal."

"Okay. The immediate *and* the long-range causes."

She shook her head. "What happened to that nice chat we were having about desserts?"

"You're not trying to distract me or anything, are you?"

"Of course not. The very idea!"

"That's good. Because if you were, I'd say it's not working."

She glanced at the doorknob, at his hand still holding it. "Try distracting yourself. Pick something and focus on it."

He looked around. He gestured toward the corner of the roof. "That post on the edge."

"Too far away. Pick something nearer."

"The smudge by your nose."

"What?" She rubbed her face with both hands.

He chuckled. "Nice going. Now you look like a raccoon."

She looked at her hands. Sooty black. They must have gotten dirty on the stair rail.

Tom watched with amusement as she searched her pockets for something to clean off with. That was so much a part of Sarah, that quality of being just a touch off-center. She always seemed to have one sleeve pushed up, or her hair flattened in one place, or a broken zipper on her handbag. Even now she was scrubbing at her face with a disintegrating tissue she'd found and only making it dirtier.

He said, "I'll do that," and took a handkerchief from his pocket.

Sarah couldn't stop looking at him as he gently wiped her face clean, at his broad chin with its barely visible cleft, the heavy lower lip . . . the blue eyes behind his smoky lenses that seemed to be laughing at her.

Then she realized what had happened.

"Tom! You did it!"

"Did what?"

"Let go of the doorknob!"

He looked at the knob, then away at the roof line, then back at the knob. He took it in both hands.

Moron! Sarah railed at herself. You might as well have walked him to the edge and told him to look down.

"Hey," she said with forced lightness, "at least go back to where you started. One hand."

He smiled but said firmly, "No."

This was getting sticky. She couldn't let him lose the progress he'd made. She had no choice but to try the flirtatious kind of joking that had gotten him up that last flight of steps.

She reached out and ran a fingernail teasingly along the back of the top hand clutching the knob. "Will you let go if I hold your hand?"

His eyes widened in surprise, and she thought he was going to take her up on it, but he kept his hands where they were and moved swiftly to kiss her.

He came so close that Sarah could smell his sweet breath before her wits surfaced and she jumped aside. He wasn't prepared for that. He slipped and tried to balance himself with his other foot, then slipped again on the roof tile and did a near somersault.

"Damn it!" he yelled, his hands still in place.

Sarah tried not to laugh and failed. In a minute giggles became guffaws. She felt terrible, but the more she tried to stop, the harder she laughed.

In a lightninglike motion Tom reached out and grabbed her arm. She tried to pull it back, but even with one hand he was strong enough to control her without even trying hard. He pulled her off her feet, brought her close to him, and then replaced his hand on the knob, so that she was imprisoned.

Sarah was furious, humiliated—and excited. She tried to duck out of his hold but he tightened it. She felt smooth skin and steely muscle. She twisted her head to avoid his kiss and found herself in an involuntary hug. Worse: it felt good. In fact, it felt wonderful.

Somehow he'd managed to trap her without letting go of the doorknob for longer than the microsecond it took to lasso her into his hold. And he showed no sign of being willing to release the knob *or* her.

She couldn't move her head without offering her ear or her lips to his mouth. He'd already shown by body language that he'd happily accept either. One of her breasts was pressed against his collarbone, the other in his armpit. Neither of her knees was in a position to help her gain her freedom. Her rear end rested in a region she dared not identify.

"Tom," she said into his bicep, "you have to let go."

"Of the knob or you?" His breath was hot in her hair.

"I'll settle for me."

Deliberately he flexed his right arm so that the motion was a brief caress on her breast. "Will you?"

Her breathing grew faster. "This isn't . . . you have to . . ."

"Turn your head, Sarah. I want to kiss you."

She couldn't stand this. She'd never felt so tingly, so enclosed in delight. His crushing hold was a drug, lulling her, dragging her under.

The next thing she knew, something irresistibly strong was gripping her head on both sides and turning it so that she faced Tom. Then he was kissing her, his mouth hot and hard on hers.

He rolled her onto her back on the sun-warmed tiles without breaking the kiss. Sarah felt his tongue meeting her own, taking possession. His big rough fingers were on her face, in her hair. They tangled in it, and he groaned against her mouth.

Blurrily Sarah knew that she was forgetting some important things. She struggled to recall what they were, but no part of her mind would cooperate. It seemed to have been overruled by her mouth and hands, which, quite without her noticing, were busy exploring Tom in the same ways he was exploring her.

It was when she realized that there were rolling knots of back muscle under her fingers that one of the things she was forgetting came clear. Hands . . . hers . . . his . . . oh, yes. His hands, if they were stroking her face and hair, couldn't still be on the doorknob, could they? That was significant. And what was the other thing?

It clicked in and jolted her back to her senses; slowly her head came unfogged, and she pushed at Tom's shoulders. The other thing was that she wasn't supposed to be doing this.

She scrambled away and pushed and pulled at herself, trying vainly to restore order, inside and out. Finally she looked up and met Tom's gaze. He was standing, watching her where she still sat on the tiles, grinning.

She said, "I didn't mean for this to happen."

He said, "I did."

Sarah spent the rest of the week in what her grandmother would have called a dither if she'd been there to see it. Luckily for Sarah, she wasn't. No new treasures arrived; no yellow Toyota greeted her at the end of a day. She was alone with her confusion . . . and her memories.

At first she'd tried to squelch the images that intruded day and night, but she soon found that was impossible. She'd be at her desk interviewing a summer job applicant . . . and out of the blue the bespectacled college student would become Tom, all sexy mouth and strong muscles, ready to imprison her again on the sunny roof. Something would appear in her face because the boy would begin to eye her warily, as though she showed signs of frothing at the mouth, and then she'd have to pull herself together and act normal again.

Or she'd be in the express checkout line at the market buying dinner, and she'd suddenly feel that mad tingle in her breast, the way she had when he'd flexed his arm to tantalize her. Her legs would weaken and she'd have to hold something for support.

Finally, by Thursday, she'd accepted that there was no way Tom would stay at arm's length now. The best she could hope to do was keep things from escalating too quickly, and even *that* would be very hard. Not just because he was attractive and sexy; that, maybe, she could have resisted. It was because that wasn't all he was. Under the commanding, supremely masculine exterior, she'd learned, was an honest-to-goodness human person. An exciting, intriguing person. How could she not be wowed by a man who had, with utter galling confidence, forced her to kiss him against her will while refusing to let go of a doorknob because he was afraid to?

Saturday came, and Sarah felt calmer. Tom had called Friday night to say a quick, warm hello before going into a late meeting. She had a feeling she'd hear from him again before the weekend was out. Meanwhile there was plenty of sunshine to enjoy—the first of the season strong enough to tan by.

From the bottom of a drawer she pulled a bathing suit she'd wadded into a ball last September, shook the wrinkles out as best she could, and put it on. She set up a beach chair on a strip of sweet-smelling grass and stretched out.

Within ten minutes she might have been on a Caribbean island. There was nothing like the first hot day of spring, when your mind and body had forgotten how good the sun felt. It was kind of a renewal.

She was starting to get drowsy. A nap would be nice but not without protection. She sat up and smoothed on a light sunscreen. Now she could relax and doze without worrying about burning.

She drifted into a dream, a Technicolor dazzler about Tom watering window boxes of petunias from an umbrella stand filled with bourbon. There was a noise, a metallic clanking. He took a chainsaw from his back pocket to prune the petunias with. The noise got louder as he worked. Soon it was so loud that he couldn't hear when she asked him to turn it off.

The sound stopped. She opened her eyes—and found a robot leaning over her, its awful metal face inches above hers. She screamed and jumped from the beach chair.

"Sarah!" it called in a muffled voice, and began lumbering after her as she ran to her apartment door.

Am I still dreaming? she wondered frenziedly. She slammed the door behind her and pushed the chain into place with fingers that barely functioned. *How does that thing know my name?*

"Sarah," it said again from outside the door.

"What—who—*are* you?" she cried.

More words came from it, too muffled to hear. It seemed to be urging her to open the door. She would as soon open it to Bigfoot. She ran to the window and craned her neck to see.

It wasn't a robot. It looked more like a knight. Or rather, like a disembodied suit of armor. It had a faceplate, and feathers curled from its head. Something tickled at the back of her mind. She watched the thing raise an ironclad forearm and bang heavily on her door.

Feathers. Peacock feathers.

"For Pete's sake!" she shrieked. She ran to the door and pulled it open. "Grandma!" She tried to push the faceplate up to confirm what was suddenly clear, that her grandmother had somehow managed to can herself in this tin thing, but Jan was too precariously balanced on her metal feet to cope with an unexpected move like that, and she teetered. Sarah grabbed for her, touched sharp points, grabbed elsewhere, and fell with her. They landed noisily on the ground in an *X*, Sarah on the bottom.

Sarah sputtered. "This is the absolute—I don't know what you could possibly . . ." She tried to catch her breath. The weight was terrific on her midriff. She realized that her grandmother wasn't saying anything.

"Grandma! Are you okay?"

Silence.

"Grandma! Answer me!"

"Glf," she heard faintly from inside the metal head.

"Oh, no. Help! Please," she shouted. "Can anyone hear me? We need help!"

She wrenched from side to side as best she could, trying to free herself from beneath the crushing weight. No one came. The parking area that on a sunny Saturday was usually busy as a Moroccan marketplace was deserted, just when she desperately needed it not to be.

She tried harder, grunting with the effort, her eyes squeezed tight. She stopped to rest. The weight was making her pant so.

A second later she could breathe. She opened her eyes. There was a pair of earth-encrusted Pumas near her head. Tom had lifted her burden away and was trying to get a better grip so as to heft it completely free.

"Don't hurt her!" Sarah shrieked.

Tom was so shocked that he almost dropped the armor. "Her?"

"That's my grandmother!"

"Sarah, what the—"

"I mean it!" She scrambled to her feet and helped him right the suit of armor on the ground. "Gently! Take it easy, she might have fainted." She pushed at the faceplate. "Grandma? Please say something."

"Your grandmother's really in there?"

"Of course my grandmother's in there!"

"Well, don't act as if I'm challenging the Holy Grail. I drive in here, find you on the ground in your bathing suit fighting off this thing—"

"She's not a—"

"*Glaaah!*" they heard from the armor.

"Thank God," Sarah said, pushing harder.

Tom said, "Don't. You could be hurting her. I'll do it." Gently but quickly he worked at the helmetlike head part. There was cloth covering her face; her blouse was stuck in the metal. That was why her voice had been muffled. Little sounds came from within, but they seemed to be encouraging rather than pained. Finally he eased the headpiece off.

"Whoo!" Jan Hellerman said, shaking her gray curls.

Tom gaped at her as though, no matter what Sarah had said, he hadn't quite believed that there was a little old lady in there.

"Are you all right?" Sarah asked, trying awkwardly to put her arms around the woman, who was still encased from the neck down. She turned to Tom. "Can't we get her out of the rest of this?"

"I'll be glad to take a shot at it. But I'd like to ask one question first. How did she get in?"

"This clearly is a man," Jan said, "who gets right to the bottom line. What do you do, dear?"

"I'm a builder."

"A builder? Oh! Then you must be—"

"Grandma," Sarah rushed in, "I'd like to know how you got in too."

"It was easy. You just step into the bottom half, then put on the top half like a jacket, then the headpiece. It's imitation, of course; the knights of old didn't have such conveniences as prefab suits. But even so, it seems to be one of those things that's easier to get into than out of. Sort of the opposite of a toothpaste tube."

70

"Are you going to tell me," Sarah said, "that you drove here from Brookline in a suit of armor?"

"Oh, dear, no, no! What do you think I am?"

"Don't tempt me."

Tom asked, "Where did you put it on?"

"In Sarah's apartment, of course."

"Of course," Sarah whispered.

"I brought it in all wrapped up. Then I saw you sunbathing from the window and decided to come out and surprise you."

Sarah thought, *I will not respond to that.*

"But," Tom persisted, "why do you have it in the first place?"

"Old Bottom Line scores again," Sarah muttered.

"It's a present for Sarah."

Sarah willed her mouth shut. Tom looked from one to the other.

"Do you think," he asked Jan, "that I could have it?"

Sarah said quickly, "You want it?"

"I'd love it."

"You would?"

"Don't argue with the man, Sarah. He doesn't seem at all unsure of himself."

She thought, *I've never had to swallow so many answers in one day in my life.*

Tom said earnestly, "I've always thought it would be great to have something like that in my place."

"That's probably hogwash, dear, but you can have it anyway. Incidentally, I'm Jan Hellerman." She held out a hinged, clanking hand.

71

He looked at it, looked at Sarah, then took it. "Tom Pagano."

"We know why I came over. How about you?"

"Uh—"

"Grandma," Sarah hissed.

"Hush, darling. You're wondering, too, I can tell. It's helpful to have someone around with the courage to ask blunt questions." She turned to Tom. "Isn't it?"

"Well—"

"But don't let me interrupt. You were saying why you dropped by."

He seemed to decide there was no point in beating around the bush. "To visit Sarah."

"Excellent reason. And a good one for me to be going."

"I didn't mean—"

"I know you didn't, dear, but I wasn't planning to stay long, anyway."

Just long enough to send me into cardiac arrest, Sarah thought.

"I'll get out of this and be on my way. No," she said as they both reached to help, "it's easier to move by myself. Heavens, what fun this was!"

Tom and Sarah watched as she clanked her way, stiff-legged, to the door and inside.

Sarah said shyly, "I'm glad you came. Thank you. I don't know what I would have done."

He grinned. "I have to admit, you're an interesting person to be around. You find cats you never lost . . . you have a grandmother who likes to put on armor and wrestle you . . ."

"Was that what it looked like? Wrestling?"

"No. It looked like you were being ravished by the Tin Man. I was ready to heave him into the bushes first and ask questions later."

"By the way, do you really want that crazy thing?"

"Why? Do you?"

"I'd rather have two broken legs and swine flu."

"That was the drift I was getting. I thought I'd help you out."

"Tom! You did that for me?"

He shrugged. "Always glad to do something nice for a pretty lady. Of course, that tends to run more to a bunch of flowers. But I thought I remembered you saying that your grandmother likes to load you up with secondhand stuff."

Jan came out in a skirt and blouse. Tom whispered, "How did she change back into Clark Kent so fast?" and Sarah giggled. They said their goodbyes and she left.

"It's nice to see you smiling," Tom said. "You looked murderous for a while there."

"I was. I love her, but I get so tired of this sometimes. Come on in. I'll make coffee."

He followed her into the kitchen. It was funny to have him really here, in her apartment, where she'd been thinking about him all week. And nice.

Tiger Lily jumped up on the table as soon as Tom sat down and began to sniff him.

"Bashful little thing," he said.

"She makes my grandmother look like a shrinking violet. She's not so little, either."

"You said it. I've seen smaller bellies on pregnant mules. What do you feed this cat?"

"German shepherds. How do you like your coffee?"

"I'll do it." He got up and took milk from the refrigerator. "Those brownies look good."

"Brownies?" Sarah wailed. "She did it again!"

"Who did what?"

"My grandmother. She makes tempting things I don't want to have around and puts them in the refrigerator when I'm not looking."

"Why don't you want them?"

"They're so fattening. She makes them with about eight pounds of butter. The calories leap out and climb my thighs."

"You don't need to worry about that. You have a fantastic shape."

He said it matter-of-factly, but the compliment delighted Sarah, anyway. She let herself buzz on it for a minute before reluctantly changing the subject. "How are those?"

"Incredible. Really rich. Only thing missing is the nuts."

"She makes them without so I'll eat them."

"You don't like nuts?"

"I like them alone but not in things. I think nuts in brownies or cookies or fudge just take up space that would otherwise be occupied by brownie, cookie, or fudge."

"I'm the opposite. In fact, when you asked the other day what my favorite dessert was, I would have said pecan pie if I ever got around to answering the question seriously. Of course, it was more fun to embarrass Miss Prim."

"You didn't embarrass me, and you should know

by now that I'm not Miss Prim," she said, and could have throttled herself. *She* meant the loony goings-on with her grandmother. But *he* was sure to think—

"No doubt in my mind. Such dedication too. There was no way I was going to let go of that doorknob for anything less than the chance to—"

"Tom!"

He grinned lazily. "Just speaking the truth. Anyway, I think I have some shorts in the trunk. I'm going to get them. Don't go away."

"Shorts?"

"Right."

"What for?" Sarah asked, feeling like her head was stuffed with hay.

"I'm going to take some rays with you."

He changed in her bathroom and spread a blanket on the grass. They spent the afternoon there, talking and joking. The sun was good and warm without being sweltering. Sarah thought Tom had about the nicest legs she'd ever seen. By the end of the day she still couldn't keep herself from looking at them every chance she got.

CHAPTER FIVE

It had cooled down to an evening crispness by dinnertime. They changed, and Sarah made barbecued chicken. When the dishes were done, they sat on the couch. For the first time since much earlier in the day, Sarah felt ill at ease. There was nothing to be busy with, not even sunbathing.

Tom said, "Have you looked at your face? You overdid it."

"I know. My back really stings."

"Got any Noxzema?"

"I don't think so."

"Vinegar?"

"Sure."

"Get it."

"Why?"

"I'm going to put some on your back."

The image of Tom lifting her shirt . . . unhooking her bra—he'd have to do that—made her face flame even redder. To cover up she said, "I'll smell like a tossed salad."

"I'll live with it."

So he was arrogantly assuming she cared about offending *his* nose.

"What are you waiting for? I'll make your back feel better in two seconds. Go on and get it."

Of course, he was right. Lily wouldn't mind, and there was no one else around.

She rummaged in a kitchen cabinet and found white vinegar, fortunately. She'd been afraid all she had was the red wine vinegar with garlic she used for salad dressings. Nobody would have been able to come near her for six months.

He pointed next to him on the couch. "Sit here and turn your back to me."

Sarah did. While she was wondering how she'd tactfully slide out of having to remove her shirt, she suddenly felt his wide hands on her. Before she could make a sound, he'd pushed it way up and was examining her shoulders.

"No problem here," he said.

"I guess I used the stronger block there," she said a little breathlessly. His hands on her upper arms, keeping the shirt in place while baring her shoulders, gripped her flesh in a hold that was all the more maddening because Tom was so detached. This wasn't feminine skin at all—merely an anonymous sunburn that needed attention.

Without warning he undid her bra.

She jumped. "Hey!"

"Shh, easy." He held her shirt up with one hand while he smoothed on the cooling vinegar with the other. He seemed to take her jump for one of surprise, and she was happy to let him. She'd have to be crazy to admit what his touch was doing—sunburn, vinegar, and all.

But why wasn't he affected? She knew he was

77

attracted to her. That warm evening on the Weyland Avenue roof had shown her that.

Or had she misinterpreted? Maybe that episode wasn't so significant in Tom's mind. Maybe they had two completely different ideas of what those torrid kisses meant. Sarah finally tempted beyond her power to remember why she was really there . . . Tom using a handy method to distract himself on a roof.

And maybe now, here on her couch, the same thing was happening, different movies unreeling in different heads. Big warm hands moving across her back in tantalizing strokes (Sarah); a good deed for the day, cooling a nasty burn (Tom). She felt a chill creeping over her that had nothing to do with the vinegar.

Her skin must have dried, because Tom let her shirt fall back into place. He closed the vinegar bottle and set it on the table. She swallowed in disappointment. It wasn't that she wanted him to try to seduce her; she was still ambivalent about even spending the day with Tom, since she was his aide above anything else. It was just so demoralizing that the man could do what he had and not be at all turned on. He must think she was the least attractive—

Suddenly he was gripping her, not from the back now. He was turning her toward him, his hold not at all like the easy touch that positioned her and held her shirt while he put on the vinegar. Happiness soared within her; she'd been wrong after all. He didn't find her unappealing. In fact, if the slight tremor of urgency she felt in his hold was any indication, unappealing was about the last thing he found her—vinegar smell and all.

He brought her near, and their faces were so close that Sarah's impulse was to shut her eyes . . . but she wouldn't. The sight of his velvety mouth moving to take hers was too sweet to miss.

She finally closed them at the last second and her other senses took over, flooding her with sensation. The smell of his skin . . . his scratchy-smooth chin rubbing hers . . . the taste of him, so intoxicating that her head spun.

He was tender at first, and her lips trembled as his moved over them. She could tell he was holding back with his kiss, trying not to be rough. But that restraint was quickly gone, and his tongue was pushing, demanding. She opened her mouth to him happily, letting in a still more dazzling rush of sensory delight.

After a few moments he held her away from him, just long enough to take off his glasses and put them on the table. Sarah didn't know she was going to do it, didn't know anything but the wants and feelings blossoming in her body, taking her over . . . but she didn't even give him a chance to hold her again before she was reaching for him. She couldn't wait to return to his mouth, his arms . . . the breathless thrill of the way he clasped her, so tight, as though to make sure she stayed there, that nothing could take her from him.

And again Sarah was borne off on the power of his kiss, tumbling somewhere away from right now, from yesterday and tomorrow. She barely knew what was happening, only that she'd never felt so many licks of flame at once, igniting all over and around her.

She was vaguely aware that she was being moved, that Tom's hands were shifting her, and the next thing she knew, she was in his lap and he was stroking her thigh—long, heavenly motions up and down. She couldn't know that while she'd been stealing glances at him all day in his shorts, admiring the way he looked, the view she'd never seen, he was way ahead of her, staring, the sight of her nearly bare body heating him up every time he looked at her. All day he'd wanted to touch her like this, every inch his to stroke and kiss. He couldn't wait to explore it all, to love her the right way. He'd show her joys she'd never imagined and fill his own hunger with the pleasure of her.

But Sarah's better judgment was prickling at her, beginning to dampen the wonder she felt. Tom's body was like a bolt of solid warmth, and she couldn't satisfy her yen for it. She wanted only more and more of him. That, she knew in the distant reaches of her mind, wasn't good.

That hand on her thigh, caressing higher now, clearly ready to breach the boundary of her shorts, was in danger of washing away what she knew to be her only course. With a tremendous effort she grabbed it and held it.

"Tom," she said. The name was unintelligible. Her voice was in such a poor imitation of working order, she could have been doing an impression of a young bear. She tried again. "Tom."

He gazed at her. She saw in his face that she

80

didn't have to explain anything; he knew exactly what was on her mind.

But he wasn't going to pay any attention. He gripped her again, pulled her to him, and went to nuzzle her ear. Once more the bouquet washed over her. His nearness was so hard to fight.

Sarah tried to get away. She couldn't move an inch, and what his mouth was doing to her ear and neck would have been an extremely effective method of political torture: to get the missile secrets he'd only have to threaten to stop.

She tried again, harder. She made no progress. He was determined not to let her go.

"Tom," she said more loudly.

"Mmm," he said, and went for her mouth.

"No!"

"Sarah . . ."

"No, Tom."

"Yes. I want you."

Using every last bit of emotional and physical strength, Sarah yanked herself away and stood. Wishing she could think of a less priggish way to put it—but surprised that her vocal cords would function at all—she said, "I'm still your aide. It wouldn't be right."

He looked at her for a long minute. He didn't buy it for a second, she could see, but he seemed to know it would do no good to push her any further.

He stood also. He reached for her and she darted away.

"Relax, Sarah," he said. He started to take her in his arms, and she stiffened. "Trust me." He stood there holding her lightly, until her body had lost its wary rigidity. Then he brushed her hair away from her ear and kissed the smooth bony point behind it.

"I'll stop—for now," he whispered. "But you're making me crazy. I won't wait long."

He kissed her mouth a final time. Sarah didn't dare say anything. She was afraid that if she opened her mouth, the only word that would come out would be, "Stay."

"Pagano."

"Tom, it's Dave. We've got another hang-up over here."

Damn it. He knew he'd regret putting in the low bid on this job. It had been trouble from the start. "What now?"

"The ducting. Rayburn said it wasn't good enough, so I reinforced it. It's stronger than a fort, but he's still bellyaching. I can't get rid of him. He's hell-bent on dragging you up here."

Tom bit down on a pencil. Leave it to a jackass like Rayburn to find some reason to get him onto a ten-story roof. He was the nit-pickingest building inspector in town, bar none.

"Okay, Dave. I'll be there in the morning."

He slammed the phone down and began to pace his office. The week was moving downhill. Too much pressure; too many things competing for a piece of his mind.

For a long minute he wished his life could be the way it used to be—before Sarah. It had been straightforward and uncomplicated. Boring sometimes, but he could always find a way to break the

82

routine; a way that didn't cause his insides to churn with such a potent mixture of feelings—as Sarah did.

Sarah. She was on his mind all the time now. Leaving her on Saturday had been about as easy as climbing a cliff. That had been only four days ago, but several times he'd had to stop himself from picking up the phone, just to hear her voice.

It wasn't good to need somebody that much. Especially for more than one reason. It had bothered him enough that he couldn't go up on a stupid roof without her. Now he needed her even more because—because she was Sarah.

Should he call her about this new problem or not? He couldn't think why he ought to, but he also didn't see how he was going to get himself up ten floors to an unfinished roof, walk around as though nothing was the matter, and take a good enough look at the ducting to convince Rayburn that it was sound.

True, he was better at heights now when he did them with Sarah—but not that much better. And the most frustrating thing was, the progress didn't seem to carry over to the job. He'd been lucky; for some time he'd been able to get out of going up on buildings. There was almost nothing his foremen couldn't handle. But Rayburn was a fiendish old goat. Tom knew his luck had run out.

What was he supposed to do, bring Sarah to work with him like a Seeing Eye dog?

He buzzed for coffee. By the time he finished it, he had an idea. A lousy idea. It was dumb and embarrassing. He thought he might prefer to wrestle a large alligator than to carry it out. But it was an idea.

He dialed Sarah's number. She sounded so happy to hear from him that he found himself grinning into the phone like a jerk. Immediately he forgot everything that had caused him to stomp around his office earlier, about needing her too much.

He asked if she could get free tomorrow.

"I think so. I'm pretty well caught up."

"Good. How are you as an actress?"

"An *actress?*"

"Not Shakespeare. Not even Brooke Shields. I need you to be a banker for a half hour or so."

"Will I have to sign autographs?"

He chuckled. "All you'll have to do is walk around frowning like a loan officer."

"Where?"

"In—on—a building we're putting up."

"On. You mean the roof."

"You got it."

"I think I see. . . ."

"I'm sure you do."

"Well, I'll be happy to do it. But I don't know anything about being a loan officer."

"You don't have to. Just look important and say 'mm-hm' a lot. The story will be that I've asked you to finance a project, so you're checking this one out."

"Sounds easy enough."

They met the next morning at Muffin Mary's near Columbia Point. Tom ordered bacon and eggs; Sarah decided she had to splurge sometime and had a mushroom omelet. When the waitress came around with the muffin basket, she took a blueberry and a cherry.

"That's the most food I've ever seen anywhere near you," Tom said. "There isn't that much in your kitchen."

Sarah shrugged. "Most of the time I watch what I eat. The only trouble is, when I decide to treat myself, I can't seem to be sensible about it. Look at this. Enough starch and cholesterol to bury a whole floor of an old folks' home."

"Speaking of old folks, I enjoyed meeting your grandmother. I think."

Sarah laughed. "That's about as positive a reaction as people ever have. She's a character, isn't she?"

"Sure is. You seem a lot more philosophical about her now than you were on Saturday."

"Oh, good grief. That idiotic suit of armor. She just shows up with one useless thing after another."

"Well, that must have set a record."

"Nope. You wouldn't believe some of the things I have. A wooden butter churn . . . I don't know what they ever cleaned it with, but it smells like a crypt. A printing press, for heaven's sake. Well, at least she didn't put those on and scare the life out of me. Oh! I forgot to thank you again for taking the armor."

"No problem. Believe it or not, it looks kind of nice in my den."

"I'll tell Grandma you put it there. She'll be thrilled."

"What do *you* do with all those things? You don't have much space."

Sarah buttered a muffin. "I use some of the more reasonable stuff. Occasionally she does bring me something that was made in this century. Mostly I put it away. There's a storage room in the building. I have everything in it but a cigar-store Indian. And she'll be showing up with one of those any day."

"Doesn't she notice that some things are missing? You'd think a printing press . . ."

"No, that's the saving grace. I don't know whether she's being polite or she forgets, but she never seems to notice that most of the things she gives me disappear."

"Probably it's her memory. She looks great for eighty, by the way."

"That's because she's seventy-six, remember?"

"Oh, yeah. That's the craziest thing I ever heard. Never mind armor and butter churns—what old lady would add four years to her age?"

Sarah pushed her shiny hair behind her ears. "She started doing it a year ago. She gets the biggest kick out of it."

"But *why?*"

"She says she can get away with whatever she wants if she's eighty. If she forgets someone's name or a doctor appointment or what she promised to bring to a church supper, she just says, 'I'm eighty, you know,' and they smile. It gives her a perfect alibi for everything. She can lecture people, argue, and demand her own way, and nobody gets mad. After all, she's eighty."

86

Tom shook his head admiringly. "What a scam."

"And you can guess what she does when she gets caught at it."

"What?"

"She says she forgot how old she was."

Tom paid the check, and they drove to the building in his car. It was nearly completed, Sarah was glad to see; she hadn't known what to expect. Her yellow knit dress wasn't quite the thing for walking through flying sawdust, and she hadn't looked forward to pulling off any kind of an acting job while she and Tom tiptoed across bare girders.

Tom took a hard hat and gave one to Sarah. She tried to put it on as though she did it all the time. She must not have looked as practiced as she thought. Tom was struggling not to laugh.

"What am I doing wrong?" she whispered.

"Nothing much. Only blinding yourself," he whispered back.

Sarah pushed the hat off her face. He was right. *She* knew she could see, but she probably looked like Beetle Bailey.

They went up in the elevator and climbed a few steps to the roof. A dark-haired, very tanned man came over and greeted Tom.

"Dave Perez, Sarah Foster from Boylston Federal," Tom said.

"Nice to meet you, Ms. Foster."

"My pleasure."

"I'm the foreman. Anything I can show you, just let me know."

He seems to know what a loan officer is here for, she thought. *Good. That makes one of us.*

Was she supposed to say anything? She felt like the only player without a script. She did the only thing you can do when you don't know your lines. She coughed.

Perez nodded knowingly. "Plaster dust. Want a handkerchief?"

"She's okay," Tom said curtly.

She was, but she suspected that the feeling wasn't mutual. She'd heard something in Tom's voice that indicated he was having trouble. It was so slight that she'd never have picked up on it if she didn't know his signals.

She thought fast. "Why don't you show me the, uh, feature we were discussing on the way up," she said.

"Right away. Dave, I'll check the ducting in a minute." He turned his back on the area of the roof where the end was visible and led Sarah to a more interior part.

"Thanks," he said. "How did you know?"

"My remarkably perceptive insight. And it also gave me a hint when you collapsed in a dead faint."

He laughed. She was glad to see that he was keeping his sense of humor. They should get through this just fine.

"I have to look at something with Dave," he said.

"What do you want me to do? Just follow?"

"That's it."

"Should I make intelligent noises about balloon payments or whatever?"

"Uh, no, thanks. Don't say anything."

"Oh, gee, Tom. Just because I put this thing on like a sailor hat—"

"More like a lamp shade. You must be a riot at parties."

"Why don't you invite me to one and find out?"

"I intend to. A small one."

"Oh?"

"Very small. Just you and me and some moonbeams. You should see how they reflect off the water and right into my place."

Sarah reddened. That wasn't what she'd meant. She was just being playful, remembering how well it had distracted him that other time on a roof. Of course, that other time on a roof had ended up just as this might have if there weren't so many people around.

Tom turned and walked off, and Sarah followed. There was tension in his upper back, in the way he held his wide shoulders, but otherwise he showed no sign of difficulty.

She watched as he and Dave Perez examined some giant square pipes. Tom made a few notes. At one point he gripped a rail as if he were only resting his hand there, but Sarah saw the skin whiten.

She followed again as they moved to another part of the roof, closer to the edge. She could see Tom trying not to look over there. Dave turned away for a minute, and Sarah took the opportunity to grab Tom's hand and give it a quick, encouraging squeeze. He shook out of her hold right away.

She felt a dart of hurt, but she reminded herself of what Tom must be going through. She resolved not to touch him again. He'd wanted her just to be there; that was what she'd do.

"So it looks okay to you?" the foreman asked.

"Stronger than a fort, just like you said. You could be safe from fallout in there."

Tom moved toward the roof door.

"You'll talk to Rayburn?" Perez said.

"Talk, hell. I'll tell the old clown he doesn't know ducting from sewer lines. Just keep doing what you're doing. I'll see he stays off your case."

Sarah and Tom went inside and down the steps to the elevator.

"That," he said, "was an asinine thing to do. Taking my hand. You might have blown everything."

Sarah glared. "Don't be silly. Nobody saw."

"How the hell do you know?"

"I made sure no one was looking."

"You don't know who's looking with that many people around. The whole point of your coming up on the roof with me was to keep my men from finding out about my fear of heights. Don't you think it was slightly dumb to grab my hand as if I were a trembling five-year-old?"

Sarah was getting angry. What gave him the right to dress her down? "I was only giving you moral support. You're acting as if I whipped a straitjacket out of my purse and put it on you."

"Don't give me that, Sarah. You did a stupid thing and you know it. Just be sure you don't do anything like it again."

They left the building and got into the car. Tom's face was tight, and he took the Pontiac into traffic with a heavier foot than usual. Sarah itched to tell him off, but she made herself keep quiet. She was his aide, and he'd just been up on a roof.

Tom glanced over at her. He was trying to calm down. His mind was a buzz of jumbled feelings. She looked so good to him, sitting there in the car . . . but that number she'd just pulled deserved a prize for rotten judgment. He didn't know whether he wanted to hug her or toss her down a well.

He dropped her at Muffin Mary's, where she'd left her car.

"Work session tomorrow," she reminded him. "Bring the suit of armor. I'll wear it to help me remember to keep my hands to myself."

They grinned at each other, but Tom's heart wasn't in it. He went to his office and returned a few calls. He got Rayburn on the phone and just about pinned the hostile old crocodile to the wall. Rayburn agreed to pass the ducting. No surprise. Tom had put all his turmoil into the battle, he knew, every enraged word that was meant for Sarah, for the workshop, for the whole idiotic problem.

The more he thought about what had happened that morning, the madder he got. Sarah had taken one hell of a chance without even considering the consequences. What on God's green earth would he have done if Dave—or, worse, one of the workmen—had seen the "banker" squeezing his hand? He'd be in an unthinkable mess if people found out he was in the workshop.

And there were plenty of ways that could happen; he'd known that from the start. Some plumbing contractor's aunt could be in the group, and he wouldn't know it; word could get around.

Not that it would affect his business. Oh, no. "Let's get Pagano for this job. Afraid of heights? You kidding, man? Well, send him a bottle of tranquilizers and we'll get Curtis instead."

The only reason he'd finally decided to take the chance was that it had seemed worth it. He'd do the workshop, he'd be fine again, and the whole thing would be over. But it wasn't happening that way. He wasn't fine. In fact, he was almost as unfine as he'd been before the program.

He put in some rug time, and then some more the next day. He'd practically worn a track in the broadloom by the time he decided what he had to do. Not through Sarah, though; that would be too risky, no matter how mad he was. It would be too easy to end up changing his mind.

"I'm sorry, Ms. Foster. He hasn't been in all afternoon."

"And he didn't leave any message for me?"

"No."

"Tell him . . . oh, never mind. We must have gotten our signals crossed. Just ask him to call me, please."

Sarah hung up. The booth was hot and stuffy. She opened the door to go but closed it again. She might as well try the clinic in case he'd left a message for her there.

"No, Sarah," the secretary said. "But I think Mr.

Pagano called Vivian early this afternoon, if that's any help."

Vivian? Why would he do that? "It might be. Is she in?"

"Yes. One second."

"Hello, Sarah," Vivian said. "Didn't you and Tom discuss this? Oh, hold on a minute."

Discuss what? she wondered as cloying music assaulted her ear. The minute stretched to three, and still Vivian didn't return.

Standing in the booth, Sarah began to feel unsettled. It was so warm in there, she could hardly breathe, but she had an icy sense that something was off. Tom hadn't come for their work session; he'd left no word for her at his office or with the workshop secretary, but he'd talked to Vivian. She didn't like the sound of that. Tom loathed Vivian; he'd never call her unless he was absolutely unwilling to discuss whatever it was with Sarah. And there was no topic that fit that description that made her feel anything but nervous. Add the fact that he hadn't shown up . . .

"Sarah? Sorry. They wanted me for a consult on—"

"Discuss what?"

"Hm?"

"You asked," Sarah said, fighting the urge to snap, "whether Tom and I had discussed 'this.' What were you referring to?"

"You mean, you don't know?"

"Know *what?*"

"Well, really. I thought he'd shared this with you or I would have phoned you. He dropped out."

Sarah's heart plummeted like a cinder block. She closed her eyes.

"I didn't confront him because I assumed you two had explored the matter. You'd better call him."

A jagged edge of hurt was forming in her stomach. She hadn't expected anything like this.

"Sarah?"

"Yes."

"Is something the matter?"

Of course not. A man who is so exciting, he makes me ache all over, and whom I started out loathing and ended up dotty about, and who seemed to want nothing more than to keep kissing me for the foreseeable future, has suddenly decided that he wants nothing to do with me. And didn't even have the grace to tell me himself. What could be the matter?

But she said, "I'll call him."

She opened the booth and wiped sweat from her face with her fingers. She stayed there a minute, leaning against the folded door. Her face quickly got wet again and she rubbed it dry, but the tears kept coming.

She would not call him at night. She wasn't required to, and she wasn't going to. As Tom's aide she had to try to bring him back into the workshop, but only one attempt was necessary, and she'd bloody well make it during business hours. She'd been so stupid to let herself get involved. Look what it had gotten her. Pouchy eyes and an empty stomach; she couldn't eat a thing. Now, way

94

too late, she was going to follow the rules. It was time—way *past* time, fool that she was—to put her dealings with Tom in the right compartment and keep them there.

Or rather, dealing—singular. She only had to speak to him once more. She'd give him the regulation pep talk, and when he told her to take a hike, she'd hang up and that would be the end. She'd rather climb barbed wire than talk to him at all, but it would be over soon.

She was in her office at eight A.M. and knew he'd be in his, but some wish not to seem too eager kept her from calling until ten.

"Yes, he is. Hold on, please," his secretary said, and Sarah gripped the phone.

"Hello, Sarah."

His tone was cool, but the now familiar timbre of his voice was like warm honey in her ear. She clenched a fist. Making her own voice as expressionless as she could, she said, "Vivian told me you want to drop out."

"I do. And I have. It's done."

"Why don't we explore your feeling about it together? Perhaps we'll discover a new direction."

"What is this, a comedy routine?"

"I was simply suggesting—"

"I've never heard you talk like that. You sound like you're doing a takeoff on Dr. Joyce Brothers."

Sarah would get through this if it pulverized her. "We customarily try to help people who want to drop out to redirect their thinking."

"Oh, I see. The party line. Well, no thanks,

there's nothing I want to redirect, except a few ideas of yours."

"Then I'll accept your decision as final. If you should change your mind, please feel free to—"

"Sarah, will you put a lid on it? Quit sounding like a recorded announcement and let's talk like people."

"I have nothing else to say. Good—"

"Don't hang up, damn it!"

She did.

She started to rub her eyes but remembered her mascara just in time. She settled for her head instead, rubbing slow circles over her temples. She'd read that it reduced tension headaches. She had one now that would win a prize at the county fair.

And her eyes were stinging. That was all she needed. One way or another, it looked like her makeup was going to end up every place but where it had started today.

Her phone rang, shocking her back to composure.

Linda said, "Tom Pagano on two."

Sarah thought, *I've had enough of this.*

Just as she picked up the phone, he said, "I told you not to hang up."

"That's too bloody bad. But I don't have a patent on rudeness. You left me standing downtown outside that building waiting for you."

He was quiet for a minute. "Well, at least you're back to English. Look, I'm sorry about that—I thought the clinic would let you know before you left for the session. But I want to put this behind us now and continue as we were."

"Continue . . . ?"

"Seeing each other. Without the phobia stuff."

"No."

"Sarah, don't be a dope. You know you want to."

Later she'd wonder how the conversation might have gone if he hadn't been so insufferably sure of her feelings. But that crack had done it, washed out the last traces, if there were any, of her ambivalence.

"I don't want to," she said. Her voice was calm and even; heaven knew why. "It would be a big mistake—for both of us. *You're* the dope, Tom. Some great things could have come out of our professional relationship. As for the other . . . well, it wouldn't work if we just picked up there. I could never be involved with you with that other thing dangling there, unresolved."

"That's moronic reasoning. When two people—"

"Oh, spare me the Adam-and-Eve philosophy!" she yelled, and hung up again. He didn't call back.

CHAPTER SIX

Sarah was glad she'd brought a book. The magazines in the law office had been chosen as if to honor every corny joke ever made about reading matter in waiting rooms. But she wished her grandmother would finish up. She didn't want to take a very long lunch hour. So far this had been one of those Mondays when it seemed as if every unemployable hard-core in Boston had woken up and said, "Today I'm going to get a job."

She read another few pages. The plot was good and scary; beings from an ancient world were coming back to life, and when they attacked someone, that person became a cunning murderer. But he didn't look different, so no one could tell the good guys from the bad. Your neighbor could pick up his hedge clippers and dismember you on your lawn.

She was so into the story that she jumped from the couch with a gasp when her grandmother touched her shoulder. She hadn't heard her come out.

Jan said, "That must be another one of your

horror books. I can always tell. Someone says hello and you faint."

Sarah smiled. "How did it go?"

"Fine. He said the new tax laws won't affect my trust fund."

Too bad, Sarah thought wryly. Though she was certain that if her grandmother had to economize, garage sales would be the last vital necessity to go.

"Thank you for coming with me," Jan said, pushing the elevator button.

"I'm always happy to. No problem."

"Yes, it is. I know it is. It means you have to zip back to ProTemp and chomp down some dreadful little bit of lunch while the clock ticks away. . . ."

"Oh, Grandma. I don't work in a penal institution."

"Well, in any case, I'm glad you came. Usually I don't mind doing these things alone, but sometimes I get tired, you know."

"Yes, I know. You're eighty."

The tenth-floor indicator lit up, and the elevator doors opened. Five people were inside. Sarah and Jan got on.

After a moment Sarah whispered, "Oh, no."

"What, dear?"

"I'm . . . afraid."

"Well, for heaven's sake, let's throw the stupid book away. I can't understand why anyone enjoys being scared. Try *The Wind in the Willows* or—"

"No, no. I'm afraid of the elevator."

"But you *teach* that."

"Shh. I don't teach people to be afraid."

"You know what I mean."

"Of course I know what you mean. It was a joke. I'm trying to distract myself." Sarah clenched her fists to stop the trembling. "I don't believe this is happening. I haven't had a problem in an elevator in two years."

The elevator was crowding up. People were turning to see what all the urgent whispering was about.

Suddenly Jan said loudly, "Pregnant woman. Excuse us, please."

"What?" Sarah hissed.

"Hush. Poke your belly out."

"This is insane! What do you think you're—"

"Stop the car at the next floor, please!" her grandmother shouted authoritatively.

Someone must have pushed Emergency Stop, because the elevator jolted to a halt and a bell sounded, loud enough to summon help from Oregon.

"Please let me be dreaming," Sarah said weakly.

"Do you feel any better?"

"Are you crazy? I was panicking because I was in an elevator. Now I'm in a *stuck* elevator."

"Well, make an honest woman of me, at least. Try to look as pregnant as you can."

"And just how am I supposed to do that? Besides throwing up, which I'm going to do, anyway, in about thirty seconds."

From the front a man said, "Ma'am, I'm a physician. Can I help?"

People shifted as best they could to let him move back to where Jan stood with her arm around Sarah.

100

A man's voice asked through an intercom, "What's the problem in there?"

Before anyone else could answer, Jan called, "The elevator is stopped. Can you move it to the next floor?"

"Sure can. Just give us a minute. The next floor is the ground, by the way. No need for anybody to panic."

Sarah went into a fit of coughing.

Someone shouted, "Call an ambulance."

Sarah and Jan yelled together, "No!"

The man who'd said he was a doctor looked at Sarah oddly. "What's the trouble?" he asked.

"She's *pregnant*," Jan repeated, as if that explained everything.

"Why is she coughing?"

"How should I know why? You're the doctor."

"Pregnant women cough for the same reasons other people do."

"Well, all I know is, we must get her off the elevator immediately."

Sarah clenched her hands tighter. Her grandmother was contemporary in so many ways, but she came from a time when the mere fact of a pregnancy could cause people to go scurrying for smelling salts and boiled water.

Sarah said to the doctor, "I'm not—"

"—well," Jan put in. "She isn't well at all. Maybe you ought to give her something."

"I don't want anyth—"

"What do you expect me to give her? The young lady looks like she could use a dry martini more than anything I have."

The elevator started with a mammoth rumble, and Sarah groaned. Everyone else cheered.

As they got off the doctor asked Sarah, "Okay now?"

"Fine!" She gave him a big smile. All she wanted was to convince everyone that she was all right and then get the heck out of there and strangle her grandmother with her own pantyhose.

A workman yelled, "Who needs the ambulance?"

Jan started to answer, but Sarah clapped a hand over her mouth and walked her outside.

Jan said, "I was only—"

"Shh!"

They got into the car.

"I wouldn't actually have let anyone put you in an ambulance."

"Oh, good."

"Sarah. Are you being sarcastic? You know I'd never go that far."

"I don't know anything of the kind." She started the Buick and took off with a screech. "I wouldn't put it past you to let someone perform brain surgery on me. What was all that pregnancy business, anyway? They're no longer auditioning for *Gone With the Wind.*"

"It was an attempt to solve the problem. Quite an intelligent one, in fact. If some fool hadn't pushed the stop button, it would have worked nicely. We'd have gotten out at the next floor and walked the rest of the way down, and the trouble would have been over."

"But the next floor was the bottom."

"Well, I didn't know that. Did you?"

Sarah had to admit that she hadn't. She'd been too busy having a nervous breakdown to watch the floor indicator. Exactly the wrong thing to do, of course. The numbers would have kept her focused on reality. She wouldn't have gotten so panicky.

"What are you going to do now?" Jan asked.

"Drop you at your car and go back to work."

"I mean, about the elevator problem. Is it a problem again, do you think?"

"Ugh."

"Does that mean yes?"

"It means that I wish I'd never gotten up this morning, and I may not tomorrow."

"I'm sorry, dear."

"Not a tenth as sorry as I am. I never thought it would come back."

"What about helping that man of yours with his roofs? How will you do that?"

Sarah pushed her bangs off her brow. "That . . . won't be an issue."

"Oh?"

"Oh."

There was a silence you could freeze and slice. Sarah tried madly to think of another topic. She simply didn't feel like discussing Tom on top of everything else.

But her grandmother's ear had been fine-tuned over the better part of a century. "Why is that?" she persisted.

Sarah sighed. "He dropped out."

Jan frowned. "That's surprising. It looked to me two weeks ago as if he were just dropping in."

103

"Out of the workshop, I mean."

"Oh. But not out of—"

"Yes. That too."

"I see. Watch it, dear. That truck was awfully close."

"Sorry."

"Well, I can see why he might give up on the roof business. It must be hard for a man. Not in the rule book, you know." She chuckled. "But he certainly wasn't behaving as though he intended to stop seeing you."

Sarah stayed silent.

"Or didn't he stop?"

The lunchtime traffic was murder. She angled out of a clogged lane and shot down an empty one, only to have to brake to a halt behind a van with its flashers on.

"Hell," she said.

"Or didn't he?" her grandmother repeated patiently, and when she got no reply, said, "I thought so."

"What? What are you talking about?"

"You know, Sarah, sometimes you . . . I don't mean you personally, I mean one; sometimes you think . . . you're not getting what you want. When what you really need to do is take another look at what that is."

Sarah had no tolerance today for her grandmother's verbal jigsaw puzzles. Fortunately there was the Toyota, just down the street. She kissed her good-bye and went back to work.

Her panic attack in the elevator hadn't been a fluke, Sarah realized as the days passed and the old aspects of her phobia trickled back. Her trouble wasn't as severe as it had been two years ago, but it could snowball if she didn't get cracking on controlling it.

She felt so down, though. She'd really thought the fears were gone for good, along with the old, needy Sarah. It could only be all this upheaval that had done it—the guilt she felt for not being able to help Tom, and her sadness. She missed him awfully. She hadn't felt this insecure in years.

Reluctantly she began working with an aide. This old problem would take time and effort to beat, but she'd make things that much tougher on herself if she tried to do it alone. She simply had to swallow the revulsion she felt about being dependent again. Since she'd become an aide herself, she'd grown used to being the one leaned *on*. It was so hard to turn back.

She found, though, that if she practiced by herself every day, she could get away with having only occasional sessions with her aide. And within a week she at least tolerated elevator rides, even if she wasn't really comfortable.

Windowed elevators were the hardest, as they'd been before. It was strange; being up high never bothered her, but going up or down, especially if she could see things pass as she went, made her nervous.

She rode the windowed elevator at the Howard Johnson's Motor Lodge in Kenmore Square every other day. When that started to get familiar, she went to Cambridge and used the one in the Hyatt-Regency. But that was less challenging, since the car ran up the middle of the pyramid-shaped hotel.

After two weeks there was just one real hurdle left: the Piermont Building on Essex Street. It had the only outside elevators she hadn't ridden, one on each side. At twenty-five stories it was more than twice as tall as either of the hotels.

There was only one trouble. Tom's firm had built it. He'd mentioned that once when she'd been talking about her own phobia work. Of course, it was probably stupid to consider that a problem. Most likely she was using the worry that she might meet Tom to cover her cold feet about the elevator. But just to be safe, she waited until six-thirty P.M. before parking across from the Piermont. He had business in his buildings from time to time, though generally during working hours.

Sarah turned off the ignition and sat in the car looking across the street. Despite her efforts to keep Tom out of her mind, a door opened in her thoughts. She couldn't help it. Maybe if it hadn't been such a beautiful building . . .

He'd said he loved it. She could see why. The restful white-gray, softened by the lowering sun . . . the tall, graceful windows . . . and the entrance, a stunning blend of black glass and chrome trim.

The mixture of classic and trailblazing designs was so typical of Tom . . . a mixture himself. Always in charge, headstrong, stubborn; then, just when you thought there would never be a break in the fence, he'd say or do something that showed the sensitivity of the stylist he was.

But that had to be a smaller part of him than she'd thought before they broke up. If he wasn't ninety-nine percent pigheaded ego, they *wouldn't* have parted; he'd have had the courage and sense to stick with the workshop instead of giving up out of embarrassment. He wouldn't have had to convince himself that he didn't need her as his aide. That showed an immature attitude.

But, oh, what she remembered . . .

She took a couple of slow breaths and tried to calm down. It wouldn't be good to get upset now. She wanted to be as relaxed as possible on the elevator.

That thick, dark hair filling her hands . . . the eyes that missed not an inch of her . . . his lovely mouth with the strong lower lip that was so delicious on her own mouth, her face . . . that had promised so much for everywhere else, promises that would never be honored.

Oh, stop. Sarah lowered the window she'd just raised and inhaled the June air. She had to get herself in gear.

She turned toward the nearer elevator and concentrated on it. She left the car and looked at it some more. Then she went into the building and got on.

Fortunately it was early enough, so the elevator wasn't empty; people stepped on and off frequently as it rose. She kept her back to the windowed part for the first fifteen floors while she mustered the courage to turn around. Finally she did it. She made herself watch the neighboring buildings recede as the elevator climbed the last ten stories.

But when it started down, she suddenly felt very different. Anxiety washed over her. She turned around, away from the window. She wished she was near enough to a side wall to hold one of the rails, but there were people in the way.

She closed her eyes, remembered that that would only increase the fear, and opened them again. She gazed around the car, trying to find something to focus on that would distract her.

At the sixteenth floor she found something. The doors opened and Tom got on.

He didn't see Sarah. He stepped into the car and stood with his back to her. But his mind must have taken a picture his eyes didn't see immediately, because suddenly he turned and looked piercingly at her.

Sarah was torn by currents of feeling—the entrancing tug of his dark blue gaze, her jittery sense of what was behind her. At last she saw comprehension in his face; he'd remembered about her trouble with outside elevators, seen her fright, and put it all together. He'd figured out why she was there. She was sorry and glad. She felt acutely embarrassed and euphorically relieved.

Without looking to either side Tom pushed through the crush of passengers to Sarah. He put his arm around her shoulders and held her tightly against him. They finished the ride in silence. After a few annoyed glances at Tom's elbowing the other riders paid no attention to either of them.

They reached the ground and got off. All Sarah could think of to say was "I was sure I wouldn't run into you."

"Meeting just broke up," he said. But the casual words masked a turmoil as great as Sarah's. He felt swamped by a wave of emotion.

In the three weeks since they'd last talked he'd been thinking of her all the time. If it had been up to him, they never would have split in the first place. But her terms—love me, love my workshop—had been impossible.

Now, though, it looked as though the tables had turned. Sarah seemed to be having trouble. He was surprised at how sorry he was for her. He felt terrible that she was suffering. He wanted to shield her, protect her.

Well, maybe he could—somewhat, at least. He'd been making himself go up on roofs, and he was getting better at it. He didn't see any reason he couldn't help her get over what seemed to be deviling her now.

And besides . . . she'd felt so good. So right inside his arm, like a vital part that had been missing. He'd hated to release her when the elevator reached the ground.

He couldn't take his eyes off her as they crossed the lobby. He remembered the taste and smell of her shiny hair, and he watched the breeze stirred by the big doors fluff it around her shoulders. Her walk was so sweetly familiar: the way she kind of bobbed, enthusiasm in every step. He thought back to the feel of her beautiful skin, her velvety cheek next to his rough one . . . and the white-

109

hot kisses that made him breathe harder even now, remembering them.

He said, "Come home with me."

Sarah stopped walking. "What?"

"Are you stalling for time or didn't you hear what I said?"

"I heard you."

"Then let's go. I'm not letting you slip away this time."

Sarah felt a joyous lightness. She couldn't quite get herself to move again.

"What are you waiting for? If you have any other plans, break them. The only thing you're doing tonight is having dinner at a condo in Salem."

"I have no other plans." It seemed ridiculous to say anything else.

They took the Tobin Bridge to Route 1A. Sarah felt as if she couldn't catch her breath. She'd read stories about people who'd been cryogenically frozen, preserved in ice to be "revived" months or years or ages later. That was how it was now: as if she'd come back to life after some long, numb interruption.

She was exquisitely conscious of the fact that this was the first time she'd been in the Pontiac for anything other than workshop purposes. Of course, she'd sat here often, having secret thoughts, the kind that had nothing to do with their professional relationship . . . but for a long time she hadn't even been willing to admit that she was attracted to Tom. And besides, it was so unlikely that he'd be interested also, it had been like watching a Redford movie.

Now the movie was really happening.

during affectedly remarked frowning. *Inbred,* maybe, *from the line. Well, Richard had been too ambitious. Richard never*

Now that he knows you'd happily..

CHAPTER SEVEN

His condo development was even nicer than she'd expected. Attached town houses of smoky wood rose in graduated heights by the water. Each unit had lush grass and artful plantings.

"Naturally I took the best one myself," Tom said as he unlocked the topmost unit. Sarah followed him inside, and her eyes widened. The whole asymmetrical wall that faced the water was glass, with a terrace cleverly done so as not to block the view. The living room seemed perched on the Atlantic. The muted sea-foam colors of the floors and walls heightened the effect.

"It's so beautiful," she said, feeling like a nerd. She wished she could think of a brighter way to express what she felt. Everyday words didn't seem sufficient. But she was still dazed by everything that had happened.

She heard a loud squeak, and Spot came running in from another room. Tom scooped him up. "My welcoming committee. He does this every night," he said.

Sarah scratched the kitten's head. "He grew so much in just two months. And look, he's getting tabby stripes. You won't be able to call him Spot anymore."

"Oh, yes, I will."

"But it doesn't fit him."

"It fits what he did to the carpet."

"Oh, no."

"He must not have been mothered much. It took him a while to get a perfect score on using the box. But now he's a gentleman. Mischievous, though. He gets into everything. Here." He led Sarah to the couch and put Spot beside her. She didn't know whether the kitten remembered her or just liked shoulders, but it promptly crawled onto hers. "Keep each other company while I get us a drink."

He was back in a minute with a bourbon for himself and a glass of red wine for her. He sat on the couch and leaned back against the dark turquoise cotton.

"Do you want to talk about the elevator?" he asked. "Or should we just be glad it threw us together and leave it at that?"

"Let's leave it," she said.

"Sure? Maybe I can help. I'm having an easier time now."

Sarah felt a jab of envy. How ironic. They broke up because he couldn't stand to have her help him . . . and now he was offering to help *her*.

"I've been up on roofs a few times," he said, unable to hide a note of pride.

It occurred to her that he was probably lying. He was unlikely to have progressed that well on his own. She began to feel uneasy; the last thing

113

she wanted was for Tom to think that he had to keep up a front for her.

But she pushed the feeling aside. The weeks without him had seemed to have no finish; all she really wanted was to enjoy being near him again.

They talked quietly and watched the water. After a time Tom said, "I'm going to defrost dinner. Want some more wine?"

"Please." She thought a minute. "Did you say defrost?"

"That's right. If you're wondering why I'm starting it so late, you must not have a microwave."

"Oh. No, I don't. Do they work that fast?"

"You can have a frozen steak ready to cook in a few minutes."

"Really? That's fantastic."

"Of course, that's if you have a steak in the freezer to begin with. It defrosts and cooks, but it doesn't shop for you."

Too bad. Sarah had already begun the calorie arithmetic, deciding where she'd skimp tomorrow to make up for a nice hunk of steak tonight.

Declining Sarah's offer of help, he went into the kitchen. She could hear dinner-preparation noises. She hadn't expected much of an appetite—the warm pleasure of being here, after having steeled herself to Tom's absence, seemed to have banished everyday concerns like dinner—but she was famished. It must be that one hunger inspired another.

She sipped her wine and watched the water some more. The food smelled great. It was hard to believe Tom could cook; he wasn't the type. But he seemed to be putting out a feast.

Finally he called her in. The dinette was separate from the kitchen, overlooking flowers and some trees, thick and green with early-summer foliage. She sat in the chair he pulled out for her.

Her plate contained a big helping of peas, an ear of corn, a roll, and . . .

She didn't know what the main course was.

It was large, flattish, dark gray, and wet-looking. If pressed to guess, she would have said it looked like a pitcher's mound in the rain. It smelled like food, though. She went to cut a bite with her fork.

The fork wouldn't go through it. Maybe it *was* a pitcher's mound.

Tom got up to get something, and she tried her knife. She was sawing at the thing, holding it with her fork, when it went sailing off her plate and across the floor into a corner. Mortified, Sarah went to rescue it. She saw an orange blur from the corner of her eye. Spot!

In three leaps she beat the kitten to the food. Or so she thought; she'd grabbed it and was about to snatch it to safety when Spot sunk tiny teeth in and growled.

I don't believe this, Sarah thought. *I'm having a tug-of-war with a three-month-old kitten over an unidentified chunk of food that's going to sit in my stomach like a bowling ball if it ever gets that far.*

"Need anything from in here?" Tom called from the kitchen.

"No, thanks," she said, and held onto the food

115

with one hand while she pried Spot away from it with the other. She hurried back to the table and had just wiped it clean and dropped it back on her plate when Tom came in.

"Spot must have been looking out the window," he said, sitting.

Sarah froze guiltily. "What do you mean?"

"Did you hear that noise he made?"

Did I ever. "Yes."

"He does that when he watches the gulls."

Her stomach curled. Was that what this was? A cooked sea gull?

Tom speared his whatever-it-was with a fork, opened his roll, and placed it inside. He shook on some ketchup from the bottle he'd just brought in. He picked the whole thing up and took a bite.

Realization dawned. She'd never have thought a hamburger could look and taste so peculiar that she'd have no idea what it was . . . but there was no other answer. Weird as it was, the idea that Tom would serve sea gulls on rolls with ketchup was a darn sight weirder.

Sarah didn't know how he'd managed to get a fork into his burger, but she knew she couldn't. She slipped hers into the roll with a few graceful shoves of her fingers, added ketchup, and chomped hard.

She might as well have bitten into a snow tire. She now had something solid and unchewable in her mouth that responded to her efforts to grind it with her back teeth by grudgingly giving up tiny fragments. Those she managed to swallow, but when she tried to reduce the rest of the bite, she had no luck. Plus, her jaw was getting sore.

When Tom turned to look out the window, she took the piece from her mouth and stuck it in her skirt pocket. She worked on the peas and corn. They were hard and chewy, too, but like pudding compared to the meat.

She was coming to the end of the vegetables, chatting pleasantly but growing desperate. What *was* she going to do with the inedible hamburger? There was too much just to leave it on her plate and claim that she was stuffed. Telling the truth was out; she'd never been able to do anything but politely lie when someone's cooking was bad. She couldn't slip it to Spot. Tom would see, and anyway, unless the kitten had the constitution of a python, he'd never digest it himself.

Tom went to get more vegetables, and Sarah knew it was now or never. She looked frantically around. The window. It was the only answer.

She raised the screen and tossed the food out, flipping it like a heavyweight Frisbee, to send it as far as possible. She shoved the screen back down and was in her seat when Tom returned.

She took more peas and corn and went on talking. She felt pounds lighter with relief. As Tom was pouring coffee Spot jumped onto the windowsill and began to sniff. Oh, no. If the cat made noise, Tom might investigate and maybe spy the hamburger. For the moment she was safe—the window was inset in a wall nook and visible only to her. But what if Spot made a real fuss?

Tom was talking about a new condo development he'd be starting soon in the Glover's Landing area of Marblehead.

"I thought the whole Salem–Marblehead area was as built up as it could be now," Sarah said.

Spot began to growl softly.

"Are the units going to be as nice as this?" she went on, raising her voice to drown out the cat.

"They should be. This particular design is getting to be my trademark." He paused. "Is that the cat at the window? The birds must be in the garden again."

Sarah turned quickly. Spot was winding up for what looked like a full performance.

"No! It's the weather. Rain. There's a terrible storm coming." She jumped up, put Spot on the floor, and closed the window.

Tom said, "But look at the living room. The sun is streaming in."

"Well, you, um, know these summer storms."

He grinned. "Sure do. This place is very romantic with the rain on the roof."

She smiled back at him weakly, thinking, *If only there was a storm. A heavy one. Heavy enough to wash away a concrete hamburger. Where is acid rain when we need it?*

She helped him clear the table, but he insisted on leaving the dishes in the sink so they could go into the living room and watch the rain. Sarah tried to change his mind, even offering to wash— anything to stay in the kitchen. After all, the rain was brewing only in her imagination. But when she gave up and followed him inside, she was astonished to see dirty gray clouds bunching over the water. The light was going quickly.

"I love this," Tom said, pulling her down on the couch that faced the window wall, "watching this kind of weather from here. I love when it turns so dark, it's like night."

Sarah looked at her watch. "It'll be night in half an hour, anyway."

Tom moved deliberately closer on the couch and took off his glasses. His dark blue eyes were fastened on her face. Sarah felt powerless to move.

She thought he was going to take her in his arms, and she waited, half tense, half breathlessly glad, for it to happen. But instead he leaned over and quickly kissed her mouth. He settled back again, his eyes still intent on her.

He said softly, "I'm going to take you to bed, Sarah."

She opened her mouth and forgot to close it. He took the opportunity to kiss her again. This time he held her lips longer, touching them with his tongue in a promise of deepest intimacy.

Still, he hadn't put a hand on her. He drew back again and just watched her. She could see the beginning of the haze of desire in his eyes, and she began to breathe faster, knowing that his emotions matched hers.

There was no question about what was going to happen. She felt oddly tranquil now, not confused at all. If she'd been asked yesterday, or an hour ago, how she'd react to hearing him calmly state that he was going to make love to her, she would have predicted turmoil, an emotional battle, and

119

jumping nerves while she wrestled with the decision. But now that it was actually happening, not the smallest part of her even considered refusing him. She'd never been as doubt-free about anything as the rightness of what they were about to share.

She didn't even have to say yes. She knew Tom could see her response playing itself out in her face. And sure enough, a corner of his sensuous mouth turned up just as she thought that. He hadn't doubted her for a minute.

He was so damned sure of himself. Sure of her. She ought to resent it. But before she could muster any such feeling, he was reaching for her.

"I told you I wouldn't wait long," he whispered as he pulled her to him.

"You waited a month," she couldn't resist reminding him.

"You weren't . . . available. But I knew that wouldn't last."

"How did you know?"

She felt one shoulder lift as he shrugged. "Things usually happen the way they're supposed to, that's all."

She tried again to feel angry and couldn't. She'd been carried to this point, and that was that. If he was arrogant about his power over her, so be it. Power it was, as strong as any force she'd ever known.

With that thought something came loose in Sarah, and the part of her that was decorous and made wise choices—the side she'd always thought was pretty much her whole self—dissolved. In its place a passionate woman emerged, one who couldn't wait to touch Tom everywhere. Her hands were suddenly in his hair, sliding up and down his back, pressing him to her. He responded immediately, clasping her tighter, crushing her mouth against his.

After a moment Tom took the pillows under Sarah's back and head and threw them on the floor, supporting her with his arm. Then he eased her down on the couch. Without the cushions she was resting flat on her back. He pulled away to shift his position, and she opened her eyes; even for those seconds she missed his closeness.

He stretched out and covered the top half of her body with his, not touching, but supporting himself with a hand on either side of her. His dark hair was mussed, falling over his brow.

He lowered himself on bent arms and kissed her eyes. His lips traced the line of her nose. She felt his warm breath on her face, and it made her want his mouth again. She took hold of his head and moved it so he had to kiss her. This time the kiss was fevered, their tongues melting into each other as though they could never get close enough.

Sarah pressed on his back to bring him all the way down and then felt the heaviness of his chest on her, a lovely weight. Now his whole broad back, with its ridges and knots of muscle, was hers to enjoy, and she went wild. She barely knew what her hands were doing, as though they had minds of their own, separate from the rest of her.

Tom responded to her caresses with a husky sound of yearning and moved his upper body against hers. The loving friction on her breasts made Sarah gasp against his mouth.

He pulled away and raised himself on his hands again. The room was very dark now. Sarah realized that she could hear rain, and it got suddenly harder, the sound filling the room as a blaze of lightning illuminated Tom's face. There was a damp sheen on it, and he was breathing raggedly. The signs of his passion made Sarah tremble. She wanted his weight on her once more, his tongue inside her eager mouth.

But when she urged him back down, he resisted. "You'll have to give me a minute," he said, his voice hoarse. "You're turning me on too much, Sarah. Wild woman! You're hard to resist, even for a minute. But I had to come up for air. I want this to last."

She smiled. No one had ever called her a wild woman before. She thought she should feel mortified; probably she would later, when she thought back on all this. But for now she couldn't argue. She *did* feel wild, wanting him so, eager to touch and taste and learn every inch of him. And the fact that his desire for her was so strong that he had to put brakes on only made her want him more.

He kissed her, keeping it sweet and gentle. Sarah ran her tongue across his big lower lip.

"I've always wanted to do that," she whispered. "I love your mouth, you know."

He chuckled softly. "I didn't know. How long have you loved my mouth?"

"I—it's hard to say."

"You're blushing. Or is that a flush of passion?

122

And why is it hard to say when you started loving my mouth?"

"Stop saying that. You're embarrassing me."

"You're the one who said it first. I'm just repeating it. When?"

"I don't know when. I wouldn't admit it at first."

"That's nice. I thought I was the only one getting ideas."

"You were—attracted to me?"

"You bet."

"Before you started inviting me out?"

"Way before."

"You had a strange way of showing it."

"No stranger than your way of showing you loved my mouth. But I'm going to show you now. I'm going to show you plenty." His face turned serious. "I wasn't lying when I said I knew we'd get back together, but I didn't tell you the whole thing, either. The truth is, I missed you like hell. I thought about you all the time. And now that I have you here, I'm not letting you move an inch until I've done all the things I've been waiting to do."

A melting heat surged through Sarah at his words, at the promise they held. Then his lips were on hers once more, and she felt his hand at her breast. His caress was strong and gentle at the same time, hunger leashed for the moment. It inflamed her more. Every effort he made to control his desire only showed her what a potent fury it was.

He took his hand away. The everyday side of her that had returned briefly while they talked—the ladylike part that was capable of being embarrassed—disappeared again. She was all feeling now. She tried to find his hand to return it to her breast. But it was busy unbuttoning his shirt while he supported himself on the other arm. That done, he went to work on her blouse. In moments it was open. He pushed it aside.

He lowered himself to her again, and Sarah felt his bare chest against her breasts. He slid his hands beneath her and stroked her back hungrily. Sarah was eager for his nakedness herself. The wonderful back she'd caressed through his shirt was now open to her touch, and she explored it, learning its smoothness, the center furrow.

His mouth moved to her neck, and he kissed its pale, soft length. She felt his tongue in the crook of her underarm. The sensation was galvanizing. He seemed to be saying that there wasn't an inch of her he didn't want to know as intimately as he could.

Lost in a honeyed mist, Sarah let her hand follow the groove of his spine all the way down, inside his pants, to where the rise of his buttocks began, where the smooth flesh gave way to hard muscle. She felt him tense, and he gasped near her ear. Then a wall seemed to fall within him, and his iron control gave way. His full length was on top of her, pressing her to him.

Sarah returned his kisses with an urgency that nearly matched his. She was completely taken over by the feelings he'd stoked, powerless to control her own desire. Foggily she knew she'd never put her hand down a man's pants before, but there was no way she could stop herself from doing anything her body willed.

She realized he'd gotten up, and she opened her eyes to find him standing by the couch, shucking his remaining clothes as quickly as he could. Without a thought she did the same, sitting up to drop her blouse from her shoulders and then pushing off her skirt and panties. When she'd dressed for a hot day this morning, leaving off bra and pantyhose, little had she known that the night that lay in store would be hotter than any day.

He watched boldly as she undressed, and when Sarah saw his eyes narrow and his breathing quicken even more, she knew exactly what he felt because she felt it too. The sight of his strong, tanned body, the male beauty that would soon be part of her, was sending her to a realm she'd never known.

Tom didn't waste an instant. One minute he was kicking his shorts away, the next he was beside her, above her, one with her. Sarah watched his face. The near agony of passion she saw there, combined with the sensations his hands and body were unleashing, electrified her.

Rain thrummed the roof as they moved together. Every thrust of Tom's titanic body was a new joy, propelling Sarah to crowning peaks of sensation. A button in the upholstery was digging into her shoulder blade, but she didn't care; she wouldn't have dreamed of asking Tom to be more gentle. She adored the way his body pressed her against the velvet of the couch with all the force of his need.

125

He freed a hand from behind her back to caress her breast. Sarah moaned into his neck. When his fingers found her nipple and held it hard, her shiver reverberated down to her toes. She bit his shoulder, and he seemed to welcome it, loving her abandon.

It was nearly over for Sarah, and she didn't want that, not so soon. To slow the sweet tension she busied her hands, burying her fingers in Tom's hair, stroking his face, his wide shoulders. Tom took her pinky in his mouth when it brushed near there and nipped it. She loved how the inside of his mouth felt, a moist cocoon.

Tom's rhythm slowed just a bit, and Sarah knew he didn't want it to be over, either. He moved her arm to kiss its smooth underside, then shifted to take her nipple in his lips. When he pulled at it, Sarah felt nearly unbearable pleasure.

All at once her hands were moving down his back to his thighs and buttocks, brashly touching. That was too much for him. He grabbed her hands and pinned them over her head in one of his.

She gripped his fingers as heat built swiftly. It took her over with shocking suddenness, pushing away all conscious thought, leaving only a trembling core of feeling. Then the explosion; she was aware of nothing but bursts of flame all over and around her, inside and out, everywhere.

"Sarah," Tom said, and gripped her almost painfully. His thumbs pressed hollows in her shoulders. He drove harder, his motions rough with love, until heaven opened for him and he shouted out a last time.

"I love you," he said a moment later, still joined to her, as close as it was possible to be.

"You're bruxing, Sarah."

"Guggig?"

"Grinding your teeth. Probably at night, if you're not aware of it. I can see it in the surfaces. What's on your mind?"

Sarah took the suction tube out of her mouth. "It's not fair to ask questions I have to answer while you're putting everything but a pickax in here."

"Oh. Sorry." The dentist chuckled. "I do that all the time. Well, *is* something bothering you? Bruxism usually indicates tension."

"No. Nothing really."

"Fine." He helped her out of the chair. "I must say, you look happy. Is it love?"

Sarah's cheeks felt warm. "Well—I guess, uh . . ."

He laughed. "Never mind. You answered the question. I just hope he's good enough to deserve you."

Sarah left the office and got into the Buick. It was newly washed—nice and clean, like her teeth. She seemed to be paying a lot more attention to little things these days. She used to file her nails or do sit-ups only when she thought of it; now she found herself doing all sorts of tasks to pretty up.

She glanced at the digital clock. Nearly twelve —time to go meet Tom where they were building on Washington Street. They'd have a quick lunch, and then she'd go back to the office.

She pulled into Huntington Avenue traffic, thinking about what Dr. Doan had said. So her mouth showed she was tense. She wouldn't have dwelled on it if he hadn't brought it up, but she was. Oh, he'd been right when he said she looked happy, but something was undeniably there, simmering just under the surface . . . a nagging concern she couldn't pinpoint.

Her elevator trouble was eating at her, of course, but that wasn't it. She'd been dealing with that for weeks now, but this other thing, this feeling of being off-center, not in her usual groove, she could only trace back as far as . . . when?

She passed Essex Street and continued toward Washington, using back streets to avoid the jammed Commons. She couldn't see the Piermont Building from here, but even being within blocks of it made her feel nice. It was such an exciting reminder of Tom. Every time she practiced in those elevators his presence was there like a spirit.

Come to think of it, her tension had begun around then, around the first time she'd practiced there and the first night she'd spent with Tom.

Well, good grief. That was probably it. Here she was, ferociously in love, her pleasant, quiet life turned upside down; it was wonderful but such a radical change that it was bound to make her tense.

Stopping for a light, she laughed aloud at herself. A woman in a car next to her eyed her warily. Well, that little piece of analysis had sure taken her long enough for such an obvious thing. Did you say you were trained in psychology, Ms. Foster?

She turned onto Washington. There was Tom's unfinished building up ahead. It was fifteen stories and coming along quickly; even from here she could see how much had been done since she'd met Tom there a few days before.

She knew he was pleased with the job—and with his own participation. She'd been wrong that first night at his apartment; he wasn't exaggerating his progress. Aide or no aide, workshop or none, he was definitely more at home with heights. Better, certainly, than she was with elevators. She couldn't help being a little jealous.

She parked and went to find Tom. She felt the buzz of excitement that always came when she was about to see him. He was hard to spot among the dozens of men in jeans and hard hats, but usually if she just stood there a minute, she'd notice a familiar big body moving in a familiar way.

Kevin O'Connor, the site foreman, saw her and hurried over.

"Sarah, I tried to call you at ProTemp. Tom had a bit of an accident."

A chill washed through her. "What happened?"

"A scaffolding he was standing on came loose and knocked him against the building. They took him to Beacon Memorial."

She tried to swallow her panic. "They?"

"The ambulance. Do you want me to take you over there?"

But Sarah was already running to her car, not caring that she could trip on the dusty rock-strewn ground. It was less than a mile to the hospital, and she covered it in about three minutes of jumped lights and screeching turns. Worries battered her. How badly was his leg hurt? Was he in horrible pain? How high had the scaffolding been? Traumatically high?

She ran into the hospital lobby, looked around frantically, and saw the information desk. "Thomas Pagano?" she said breathlessly. "What room is he in, please?"

The pink-coated elderly woman picked through her file cards with maddening slowness. Her bent head looked as if someone had spread it with glue and then sprinkled on cotton balls. She shook it and began looking through another stack of cards. Sarah raked her bangs back with her fingers, worry making her stomach roll.

"I don't find it," the woman said. "Pagano with a *P,* didn't you say?"

"Yes," Sarah said shortly.

"When was he admitted?"

"This morning. He was injured. The ambulance brought him."

"Oh. No wonder, That would be Emergency, then, if he's not listed here. Around the corner, through the doors, and turn right."

Sarah had to stop two nurses and an orderly before she finally learned that Tom was in the cast room and was directed there. She hurried in and nearly cried with relief. He lay on a stretcher, very much awake, with his leg elevated on pillows. There was an ice pack on his knee, but she could see that it was huge, swollen to twice its normal size.

"Sarah," he said, and grinned and reached for

her. She was so glad he was all right. She hugged him and was thrilled to see that his grip was as strong as ever.

"I was so worried," she whispered. "You don't know how happy I am to find you all in one piece."

"One too many, damn it. Look at my knee."

She let go of him. "It sure is swollen. Is it broken?"

"Dislocated. The kneecap."

"How awful. Will you have to get a cast?"

"No. They're going to aspirate it—take some of the blood out, to reduce the swelling—and then put a gizmo on it that acts like a cast."

"Don't they have to push the bone back in place?"

"They already did."

"Oh, Tom. It must have hurt terribly. Not that you'd admit it."

"The hell. It felt like someone was dynamiting my damn leg."

"And now they're putting a needle in? It doesn't seem fair to keep hurting you. You go to a hospital to *stop* hurting."

"Those are the facts of life, unfortunately," a plump blond doctor said as she came in. "You have to feel worse before you can feel better."

"Well, can you do it? I'd like to get out of here."

"Patience, patience. Is he always in such a hurry?"

"Yes," Sarah said.

"What? I am not."

She felt like a half-wit. He looked so much like he did when they made love, with his glasses off

131

and his hair mussed, that that was what had made her answer that way. He'd said he wouldn't wait long to have her . . . and he hadn't, even though they'd stopped speaking in the interim and she'd intended not to see him again.

She turned away, ashamed of her stupid reply. Tom gripped her chin and turned her head. He gazed at her. He knew just what she was thinking. She felt her face heat up and her breathing quicken.

"I hate to break this up," the orthopedist said, "but you have a little date with a needle to keep now. Hold his hand, he's going to feel this."

Sarah watched the big needle penetrate Tom's swollen knee. A muscle in his jaw tensed, but he showed no other reaction.

"Can you put on the cast thing as soon as this is done?" he asked.

"The immobilizer. Yes, I'm going to."

She filled several tubes and removed the needle. The swelling was down. She wrapped his knee in an Ace bandage, then put on a long harnesslike contraption with big Velcro fasteners. He sat up and started to climb off the stretcher.

"Not so fast," she said. She made him stay put while she explained that the immobilizer was to be treated like a cast and removed only for showering. He was to stay in the house until he felt comfortable on crutches for long periods outside. He had to see her in three weeks; the immobilizer would come off then, or in another week. She adjusted crutches for his size and watched to make sure he could move well on them.

132

They left the hospital, Tom moving with surprising agility.

Sarah said, "I'm so relieved. I was terribly worried." She threw her arms around him.

"Ow!"

"Oh, no!" she said, jumping back.

He scowled. This was all he needed. Five jobs going and now he couldn't work. And to top everything off he couldn't get close to Sarah without his knee hurting fit to kill.

She misread his expression. "I'm really sorry. I didn't think."

"What? Oh, no problem."

"But you look like you're in terrible pain."

"Well, it hurts. But I'm just mad."

And he was, anybody could see that. Sympathy filled her. For such a strong, vital man to be helpless, even temporarily . . .

"I'm parked right over here," she said. "Should I pull the car up?"

"No. I can make it to the car, for pete's sake."

She started to tell him not to take it out on her but kept her mouth shut. She had to be patient.

She pushed the car seat back as far as it would go and kept her hands determinedly to herself while he got clumsily into it. She stuck the crutches in the backseat, started the car, and headed for the Tobin Bridge. After a few blocks Sarah felt Tom's hand on the back of her neck. He stroked her there and tangled his fingers in her hair.

"You're distracting me," she said.

"But you don't want me to stop."

She closed her eyes for a second as a shivery

feeling pulsed where his hand was. "I . . . it's hard to drive."

He leaned over and kissed the place he'd been stroking. "What difference can it make? You're some cowboy driver, anyway."

"That's what my grandmother says."

"Watch that truck."

"She says that too."

"Guess I shouldn't complain. At least I have a ride home."

"Not to mention a private nurse."

"Huh?"

"If you want one."

He settled back in his seat. "You're offering to stay with me?"

"For a while. As long as you need."

He winced at that. For a second he had an image of Sarah the helper, the way she'd been when he started the workshop—a little too eager to fuss and fret and take care of him. But another picture pushed it away. Sarah at his place . . . in his bed every night . . . the smell and taste of her, the delectable body he loved. Sarah for company, with him all the time. Her sunny ways, the laugh that came so often . . . the way she made him feel good just by being near.

It was a terrific vision, like a great dream.

"A guy would be an idiot to say no," he told her, taking her hand from where it rested between the seats and bringing it to his mouth. He kissed each finger. "What about ProTemp?"

"I'll take my vacation time. I usually go around now, anyway. Look, you'd better stop that."

134

He ran teasing fingers along her arm, up the sensitive inner surface, and beneath her short sleeve. "I think I'll keep it up. Just to make sure you don't change your mind."

She glanced at him in surprise. "I won't. Don't be silly. I want to help."

He felt uneasy for a minute, but he was kissing the crook of her arm, and her fragrance closed everything else out of his mind.

CHAPTER EIGHT

"Mostly bills for you, it looks like," Sarah said, "and a postcard for me from my grandmother. On the Cape."

"What? What about the cat?"

"She took her along. It says, 'Tiger Lily and I are having a great time.' "

"She went to the Cape with a cat?"

"You know my grandmother."

"True," he said, shifting his leg to a new position on the couch. "I guess I'd be more surprised if she went on a bus with the Golden Agers club or whatever. How do you suppose she found a motel that would take pets?"

"She wouldn't bother to ask. If they give her a hard time, she'll just look mournful and tell them she's eighty." Sarah sat down. "Whose turn is it?"

"Yours. Roll."

She threw the dice. "Six. Let's see . . . orange. What's that again?"

"Sports and Leisure."

"Oh. Well, give me a Leisure."

"You can't split it up. The whole category is Sports and Leisure. That's how Trivial Pursuit is

136

played; you have to use the categories they give you. Okay. What was Gertrude Ederle the first woman to do? You get all the easy ones."

"Very funny."

"I mean it."

"You know the answer to that?" Sarah asked incredulously.

"Sure."

The sliding doors were open, and the sea-scented breeze filled the living room, ruffling papers and Sarah's hair.

"Hm . . . was she the first woman to . . . uh . . . be a governor?"

"Remember the category."

"Oh, yes. The first to . . . swim the English Channel?"

He frowned. "Are you putting me on?"

"Well, I don't know what a good answer is, Tom. I know as much about sports as you do about lipstick. It was the only thing I could think of."

"It's right."

She clapped. "You're kidding!"

"Nope. Go again."

"Three. Pink. Is that Entertainment? I'll take it."

"What was Howdy Doody's sister's name?"

"He had a sister? I don't know. Marilyn."

"Marilyn Doody? Sorry. It was Heidi."

"Heidi Doody? I don't believe it."

He showed her the back of the card.

"Don't tell me," she said, "you knew that too."

He shook his head and rolled the dice. "Blue. Good. Let's have the Geography question."

"What country's capital is Tirana?"

He looked disgusted. "I'll take a guess. Andorra."

"Albania. Good. I go again."

"This is ridiculous. I'm the expert. You've never played before. How come you have three pie pieces and I don't have any?"

"It must be your injury."

"I don't think with my knee."

"Good, the green pie. I need that piece."

"Science and Nature. Okay." He smirked. "What's the meaning of the zoological term 'ruminant'?"

"An animal that chews its cud."

He pitched the card. "Give me a break. How did you know that?"

Sarah shrugged. "I remember it from college. It happened to stick in my mind because it made me think of 'ruminate,' and I thought that was just how a cow looked when it chews, as if it's pondering some significant—"

"Never mind. I can't compete with the kind of memory that attaches vocabulary words to cows. Roll the dice."

"Four. Brown. Arts and Literature? I'll take that."

"Who's considered the first important American novelist?"

"I think—Nathaniel Hawthorne."

"Wrong. James Fenimore Cooper."

"What? That's ridiculous. In fact, it's not a fair question. What do they mean, 'considered'? Who's supposed to be doing the considering? I might consider Stephen King to be the first important American novelist."

"Let's have the dice. Ha! Orange." He rubbed his hands together. "It's about time. Now I'm going to be on the way. Give me the Sports and Leisure question."

Sarah squinted at the card. "Which point value counts when an arrow cuts two colors of an archery target, the higher or lower?"

"Uh—the lower."

"Higher."

"That's it." He threw up his hands. "I'm getting all the asinine questions today. Put the game away."

"Quitter."

"No way. It's a matter of survival. There are times in this game when you fall into a losing groove and can't get out. You only have impossible questions. That's a fact. Everybody knows it."

"I don't know it, and I'm part of everybody," Sarah said, picking up the game pieces.

"I'll prove it. Sports and Leisure is my best category; Geography is second. Read the next question in those."

She reopened the box of cards and took one. "Sports and Leisure. What is the distance of straight-line sprints in drag racing?" She looked at the next card. "Between which two countries is the Khyber Pass? You're right. I see exactly what you mean."

He eyed her suspiciously. "Are you humoring me?"

"Would I do that?"

139

"I don't like that look in your eye. It's a little too innocent."

"Innocent? Me?" She laughed. Her cheeks were flushed. "Not in the last few weeks, anyway. Thanks to you."

The breeze had gotten stronger; some papers were blowing off an end table. Sarah got up to slide the glass door partway shut and pick up the papers. Tom watched her move in her very brief blue-green shorts and striped crop top. With her thick, shaggy, honey-brown hair and full mouth, she looked like a combination of smooth, tanned girl and exquisite woman. The shorts and top rode up when she bent, exposing still more of her sweet curves. Desire snaked through him.

"It's time I got back to maintaining that reputation," he said a little hoarsely.

She reddened again. "Not yet, it isn't. You know what the doctor said. It's only been four days."

Tough, he thought. The doctor wasn't undergoing the torture of staying immobile while a woman who made his glasses steam paraded around in an outfit he'd never let her outside in.

Not that Sarah was intentionally enticing him. She had a right to keep cool. He'd hardly make her wear a high collar and corset just so he could keep from thinking about how badly he wanted her.

It *was* cruel and inhuman, though, no doubt about it. Only his knee was out of commission. All other areas were intact and ready to function as usual. *They* didn't understand that because he had to keep the knee still for a week, they were expected to survive on a few kisses and hugs.

140

The phone rang. It was Dave Perez, needing advice about a delivery problem. He reluctantly abandoned his train of thought to discuss alternative sources of supply.

Sarah finished straightening up and went into the bedroom, pausing for a lingering look at Tom. He was so appealing there on the couch in tennis shorts and nothing else. Her hands itched to trace the hairy pattern of his stomach, caress the hard beauty of his one uncovered leg. Right there where the top of his thigh met the shorts, and the hair got thicker and curlier . . .

It was so hard to look at him without a shirt and keep her hands to herself. She remembered well how tightly his sun-browned arms could hold her. She wished she could run her fingers along them to feel the steeliness of the flexed muscle. She saw it ripple now as he shifted the phone to his other ear and reached for a pencil.

Enough. She was going to have to move to a pup tent on the lawn if she didn't find a way to distract herself. It would be only a few more days before they could really enjoy each other; until then, the small amount of touching and kissing they could manage without giving him intense pain would have to do.

She took a bottle of nail polish from her makeup case, slipped off her sandals, and sat on the edge of the bed. Even with the frustration of keeping her distance from Tom, she was enjoying her vacation time. She was getting a nice tan on the balcony, and being by the water was delightfully relaxing. The tension that had been deviling her was gone.

141

She heard the rhythmic thump of Tom's crutches as she began painting her toenails. He came into the room and stood looking down at her. A slight smile played about the mouth she loved, the full lower lip that felt so good taking hers.

"Let me do that," he said, and lowered himself to the floor. He took the brush from her hand.

"I hope you're good at it," she said uneasily.

"We're about to find out. Scat, you," he told Spot, who was sniffing around, investigating the polish.

"You mean you've never done this?"

He looked at her with aggrieved patience. "No, Sarah. I don't generally do my nails. It doesn't go over too well with my men when I show up in a hard hat and—"

"I thought you might have done some other . . . I mean—"

"Some other woman's nails? Uh-uh. This is a first." He cupped her heel in his hand and brushed kisses along her instep. "When I saw what you were doing, it was too tempting not to take over. Your feet are as gorgeous as the rest of you."

Sarah clenched her teeth, vowing not to let his touch make her feel things she didn't want to. Not this pooling warmth that stole up her leg and made her tremble . . . not the small flashes of heat where he was holding her foot and gently moving her toes so as not to smear . . .

"I hope," she said, counting on a joke to clear away the mist of feeling that shimmered between them, "that you're better at this than you are at microwave cooking."

142

He looked up. *"I* liked that chicken."

"You must be part cannibal. It was still clucking."

She'd finally worked up the nerve to be honest about his microwave meals, though she'd never be able to tell him about the hamburger. She'd retrieved it from the lawn while Tom was showering the morning after she'd thrown it there; even the night's four-legged prowlers hadn't wanted it. Spot and Lily still got very interested in the skirt she'd stuffed her unchewable bite in, though she'd washed it. But this time around she'd had to speak up or she'd have wasted away.

"The spinach was good," he said.

"I made the spinach. On the stove."

"Oh, yeah. What do you call this color? Brothel red?"

Sarah laughed. "I don't remember. The name is on the bottom of the—*no!*" she shouted as he started to turn the bottle over.

"Sorry." Nice, Pagano. The lady has you so bushwhacked, you almost poured nail polish on your carpet. "How'd I do?"

She sat monkeylike to examine her nails. They looked fine, no stray globs. "Terrific. Will you give me a second coat?"

"I'll give you anything you want, love," he said in the throaty voice he used only when they were very, very close. She felt a rush of excitement and closed her eyes to will her emotions back to a mere roar. When she looked again, he was intent on what he was doing. She watched his big fingers move; the brush was hidden in them. Carefully he stroked the bright polish over each nail, sliding the fingers of his other hand between her toes to separate them.

He finished that foot, kissed it, and gently let it go. He started on the other.

Sarah looked longingly at his thick hair, easily within her reach as he kept his head bent over her nails. She caught herself with her hand on its way to stroke it and pulled it back as if it had been bitten. He was making her feel so shivery-warm, she wanted more . . . but she couldn't touch him. It wasn't fair. If things started to escalate, as they undoubtedly would, he'd be in pain and it would be her fault.

Maybe if she didn't watch, she could get her mind off what was happening. She lay back on the bed and stared at the ceiling. Tom finished her other foot. She felt him raise her leg; then his mouth was in the pillow of flesh behind her knee, and he was running his hand up and down her calf.

She sat right up. "Tom—"

"Shh." Now his lips were where she'd longed to touch him when he was on the couch, nibbling along her inner thigh, and she was going down for the last time.

"I don't think I can—"

"Don't talk," he said quietly. "I don't care what happens. I can't take this anymore."

He kissed her through her shorts, and Sarah gasped and buried her hands in his hair. A moment later he was beside her, gathering her in his arms. Spot jumped onto the bed, and Tom put him off. He got back up. Tom ignored him and held

144

Sarah tightly to his chest, his mouth on her ear and cheek, his tongue tasting the corner of her mouth. She could feel his excitement and it boosted her own. She hugged him back, caressing the muscled arms she'd gazed at so hungrily.

Tom raised his head to look at her face. "I have some lost time to make up for," he said. "I'm going to kiss you all over—and then I'm going to take you. By the time I'm through, you'll know beyond a doubt that you're mine."

He moved down and started to pull off her shorts.

"Yowrr!" Spot screamed, and leapt from the bed.

Sarah burst out laughing. "Maybe," she said, "he thought you were going to do all that to *him.*"

Tom playfully slapped her bottom. "I knelt on his tail. If you're trying to sidetrack me, forget it. Nothing less than a tornado is going to keep me from making love to you. And the tornado would have to come through the bedroom."

She gave it one last try. "But . . . your leg—"

"The hell with my leg. There are other areas that need a lot more attention right now."

He slid his hands under her and turned her on her side so that they could lie together full-length. Sarah let out her breath in a long sigh of bliss. It felt so wonderful to be held again. His unencumbered leg was divine against hers, the hairy muscular flesh the lovely sensation she'd been dreaming of.

He stroked her hair back from her forehead. He kissed her face all over, her eyes, the side of her nose. His tongue played under her ear and behind it.

"Mmm," Sarah murmured, and snuggled against him, her body seeking all of his. He put a hand on her buttocks and pressed to bring her closer, as close as could be. Then he kissed her mouth fully, his tongue entering to claim every small corner.

After a while Sarah pulled away to catch her breath, but Tom refused to stop even for a minute. Looking into her eyes, he took her hand and pressed it to his shorts. Her impulse was to pull it away, but his eyes told her how much he wanted it there, and really, deep down, she did too.

Gingerly at first, and then more confidently, she gave herself over to new and exciting feelings, caressing him with an abandon she wouldn't have thought herself capable of. When he pulled his shorts off, she barely noticed the awkward minute it took, so intent was she on loving all of him.

Too soon he took her shoulders and pulled her firmly away—too soon for Sarah, but she knew from the urgent way he moved her that he couldn't wait an instant longer to make them one.

Pain flickered in his face, not for the first time. Part of her thought they should stop before he got hurt badly; but the other side, much more persuasive, wanted to be filled, made fully his.

She needn't have worried. She should have known that Tom's passion would find a way. Within seconds her few clothes were off and he had her placed beside him so that he could love her without moving his bad leg too much. He shifted her almost roughly, fiercely eager to be within her.

"Tom, oh!" she gasped when it happened, and wrapped her arms around him, burying her face in his neck. Had it ever been like this, so agonizingly sweet that she almost couldn't bear it? She felt supercharged with power, Tom's power. Great sheets of electric heat were invading her.

She heard him say her name hoarsely. He gripped her tighter, loving her faster and harder. His breath was ragged thunder in her ear. There was one achingly long moment of white-hot stillness . . . and then Sarah was zooming through space, lost in wonder, aware of nothing but Tom joining her seconds later. Together they reached for heaven and caught it.

Her last waking thought before they drifted into the most peaceful sleep either had had in days was that she'd probably need to do her nails again. But she'd happily have done them eight times with a whisk broom if it meant being with Tom like this.

"How about Gloucester?" Sarah said, looking up from the map. "It's not that far, and it's an easy drive."

"I don't know if I can survive you playing kamikaze with the trucks on Route One-twenty-eight."

"I'll be good, I promise. It's only fair, since you're a passenger involuntarily."

"About as involuntary as you'll ever see. Just another week and this damn thing comes off for good. I can't wait."

"It might be two weeks," Sarah reminded him. "She said three or four."

"Not if I can help it."

"Well, is Gloucester okay? We could window-shop and maybe sit on the beach."

"Let me think . . . yeah." He snapped his fingers. "There's a pond, off Dune Avenue somewhere, before the village. I'm sure I can find it. And we can rent a rowboat at a shack nearby."

"That sounds terrific," Sarah said, folding the map. "Let's."

Tom pulled himself off the couch. "Get some hamburgers and stuff out of the refrigerator and I'll pack up the barbecue."

Soon they were heading north on 1A toward 128. The July morning was clear and quiet with no haze—nothing to interrupt the sky but busy gulls and a few white touches of cloud.

"Hey," Tom groused shortly after they'd turned onto 128, "you want to slow this bomb? I had in mind another forty years or so of living."

"Was I speeding? Sorry."

"Maybe I'm being picky. But eighty-five is a little fast."

"Good heavens. I had no idea."

"With those big numbers flashing in your face?" He gestured at the Buick's dashboard. The digital control panel showed the speed in lighted green figures an inch high. "What did you do when you had a car with a regular speedometer? You must have burned up the road. Have you ever been stopped?"

"Uh, yes."

"How many times?"

"I brought hamburgers *and* hot dogs. Do you think that'll be too much?"

"Oho. She's trying to lead me astray. This must be interesting. How many times?"

"A few."

He leaned toward her. The corners of his mouth were turning up in that grin that always made her dissolve. "Number?"

"I'm not sure. Three or four."

"Oh, that's not so bad. You must be good at avoiding the law." He thought a minute. "Three or four in your whole driving career?"

Silence. "No."

"In how long?"

"About a year."

He threw back his head and laughed. Sarah rolled her eyes.

"You must not get tickets every time," he said. "You'd lose your license."

"I've never gotten a ticket."

He turned to her. "You're kidding."

"No. They always let me go."

"It must be those huge brown eyes. I guess I'm not the only one bedazzled by them."

"My huge brown eyes see an exit up ahead," Sarah said. "Is that the one?"

"Sure is. Turn right off the ramp."

He directed her through green, summer-fragrant rural roads to a big freshwater pond. There was a little vee of sandy beach for swimming and rowboat launching. No one else was in sight.

"Good," Tom said. "It's as quiet as it was when I

149

brought my sister's kids here last year. Turn left and we'll get a boat."

They left the picnic cooler and grill under a tree and slid the aluminum rowboat partly into the water. Sarah heard a car stop and turned to see a family emptying out of a station wagon loaded as if for the Sahara. Four small children ran down the grass to the beach and arranged themselves in a line to watch.

"Well," Tom murmured, "it *was* quiet. Get in and let's shove off. It's a big pond. We'll just row to the other end."

One of the children, a blond boy of about three, took his thumb out of his mouth long enough to ask, "What's that on your leg?"

"A big bandage," Tom said, "because I hurt my knee."

"*You* get in," Sarah said. "How can you shove off with one leg?"

"I can do it. Now, will you—"

"You're gonna fall," a little girl said, clearly pleased at the prospect.

"She's right," Sarah whispered.

Unpacking the wagon, their mother called, "Kids! Leave the people alone." She turned back to what she was doing. The children didn't move.

"Get in the damn boat. We're getting out of here."

"Ooh!" the girl trilled. "Daddy! *Daddy!* The man said a bad word!"

Tom helped Sarah into the boat, put his crutches in, and gave it a hard push. He grabbed the side

150

and tried to swing himself into it, but there was a quick drop in the water depth that he hadn't expected, and the hop he made to get momentum backfired. He spun and went down in a whirl of arms and legs, pulling over the boat and dumping Sarah.

They surfaced to hysterical high-pitched laughter and small hands clapping. Tom made a grab for his sinking glasses, splashing Sarah more. This was a tremendous crowd pleaser.

Tom said through gritted teeth, "Get back in the boat."

"But—"

"Get *in*. At least this time we don't have to worry about getting wet."

The children watched the boat leave and then turned away, disappointed that the show was over so soon. Tom and Sarah peeled off the sopping shirts they'd worn over their suits, and Tom propped his leg on Sarah's seat.

"You weren't supposed to get the immobilizer wet," she said.

"Gee whiz. You should have told me sooner."

"Don't be sarcastic."

"Well, it's not as if I intentionally went swimming in it."

"Sorry. What should we do?"

He shrugged. "I can't be the first person who ever fell in the water while wearing one. It'll be okay. Let's row around until we're hungry, and then I'll take it off and leave it in the sun while we eat."

They explored the pond's secret pockets and watched the birds and bullfrogs. Away from the little beach there was no sound but the oars' whoosh and the hum of insects.

Tom looked at the sky. "Time to eat."

"You can tell by the sun? I've always admired that."

He chuckled. "I can tell by my stomach. I have no idea what the sun says. I was looking at some gulls."

The station wagon hadn't left, but there were no kids in sight when they pulled the boat out of the water. "Maybe they drowned," Tom said hopefully. They spread a blanket in a private spot and started the coals going in the grill. Tom took off the immobilizer, and Sarah laid it over a warm rock in the sun.

She was unwrapping the food when, one by one, four small figures came walking around a bush.

"We smelled a fire," one said.

"Can I see your boo-boo?" another asked, squatting to peer at Tom's exposed leg.

"Ki-i-ds!" they heard.

Sarah said, "Your mom's calling you."

They stood still.

Tom pointed toward the voice. "I smell marshmallows roasting over there. You'd better go get them before the bears do."

They trotted off, and Sarah laughed. "Anyone ever tell you that you have a way with kids?"

He grinned and reached for her. "I'd rather have my way with you."

"I was just going to put the hamburgers on."

He gripped her arm, pulled her close, and kissed her right where her breasts swelled above her swimsuit. She whispered, "Then again . . ."

CHAPTER NINE

"It's been a long time," Tom said grimly.

"I know," Sarah said. "This won't be easy. But you have to try your best."

"Where to?"

"Well, let's talk about that. How far back do you think you want to start?"

"Oh, roughly square one," he said with a humorless laugh.

"It's really that bad?"

"Yes, it's that bad," he mimicked nastily. "What the hell do you expect? I had the kind of accident every guy in my business has nightmares about."

Sarah held her tongue. She had to act like a real professional now, not respond as she might have if they weren't in a work session.

"Let's start with looking out windows, then, and see how you do with that."

She directed him to an address on Hemenway Street, the same type of five-story building they'd worked in at the beginning.

They got out of the Pontiac. Tom slammed the door, and Sarah glanced at him but kept quiet.

Inside she said, "Okay. You know the routine. Up one flight and have a look out."

As she had months ago, Sarah watched his back as he climbed the stairs, the motion of his muscular legs and buttocks. Only now, what she felt was much more than absent admiration, for she knew those areas intimately, could visualize the look and feel of his nakedness. She had to close her eyes for a minute against the reaction the sight of him evoked. A languor threatened to overtake her, a fluid glow that spread through her limbs and centered somewhere low in her stomach.

Not for the first time the professional Sarah tapped the Sarah-in-love firmly on the shoulder and asked if she was quite sure she knew what she was doing. Wasn't it chancy at best and unprofessional at worst to have let herself be reassigned as Tom's aide when she could have spoken up and stepped aside? Did she really think she could forget in their sessions that he was anything but a workshop member?

And as usual, Sarah-in-love held her ground. Naturally she hadn't mentioned her relationship with Tom at the clinic. That would be indiscreet and silly. Besides, the whole point was Tom and how his needs could best be met, wasn't it? She was certainly the person most qualified to fill that role.

It would take strength for her to continue as Tom's aide without it causing any problems, but she *was* strong, much more so than she'd once been. She'd proved it in many ways. When something got her down, she always dealt with it.

Hadn't she managed to control her elevator phobia for the second time?

"Here," Tom called.

She went through the exercises with him and then told him to repeat them on the next floor. They didn't seem too troublesome, so she had him join her on the third-floor fire escape.

He wasn't a hundred percent comfortable there, but he was calmer than he'd been the first time they did that.

"You haven't lost that much ground," Sarah told him as they left the building. She felt encouraged; she wanted him to feel the same way. "And it shouldn't take you nearly as long to get back to where you were as it took you to get there in the first place."

They sat in the car. "That's a good thing, of course," she went on, "because there're only three weeks left of the program. If you *really* had to start all over again, you'd be in a pickle. But assuming you keep up the progress, I don't see any reason—"

"Okay," he said curtly. "I get the point."

Sarah was stung. "Well, you don't have to sound so—"

"Drop it, will you?" He glanced over his shoulder for traffic and changed lanes. "I understood what you were saying three sentences ago. The session is over. Let's go on to something else." He turned on the radio.

"—Red Sox as last year. They don't have one usable shortstop, know what I mean? They *stink.*"

"Thanks, Stan from Malden," the host said. "Hello, this is Sportsphone, you're on the air."

Tom pushed a button.

"—*de*-grees in Beantown, and a hot night's on the way. Say, if those pimples—"

He pushed another.

"—in the way of communication. What I'm hearing is that you wish your husband would give you more input. Now, if—"

Tom shut it off. "Doesn't anybody just play music anymore?"

"Depends what you mean by music," Sarah said.

"I'll tell you what I don't mean. Loud, screaming rock that splits your—"

"I love that kind."

He shook his head and smiled. Not only weren't they on the same wavelength today, they were so far off it was almost funny.

"I'd better get you to your car," he said, "before we pull switchblades on each other. Are we set for tomorrow night?"

"Definitely. I'm looking forward to it."

He was too. Dinner and dancing at Harbor House, the waterfront restaurant . . . they could use a night like that, he reflected as he drove up 1A after dropping off Sarah. Maybe it was the pressure of getting back to work after they'd both had those weeks off, but the honeymoon spirit, the tender joy they'd shared, seemed to have thinned.

He loved her, that was for sure; his feelings deepened by the day. He knew she felt the same. But something was out of whack. The problem was so frustrating, because if he could just isolate it, he could fix it. He hated vague trouble that couldn't be pinned down and solved.

He had great memories of the time they'd spent in Salem. Even that third week, when Sarah's vacation time was over, she'd come every night after work to help him keep the place clean and get dinner.

Sometimes he'd felt she was a little *too* helpful. But he'd pushed that away guiltily. Only an ingrate wouldn't appreciate all she was doing.

He slid the Pontiac into the parking area by his apartment, got out, and stood for a moment looking pensively at the water. The best thing he could do was try to forget the nebulous feeling that kept brushing at him like a spiderweb. There was no action he could take now, anyway. Maybe tomorrow night would get them back in the groove.

Sarah giggled. "Look at the menu. I guess this is supposed to be a Colonial touch, substituting *f* for *s*. It looks so funny, though. Should I have filet of fole or ftuffed fhrimp?"

Tom grinned. This was the Sarah he was crazy about—all fun and loveliness. No cause, no goal, no earnest take-charge attitude. He'd been right. This evening was a good idea.

He ordered for both of them and asked for the wine to be brought right away. "It's red," he told Sarah. "I think you'll like it."

"I love red wine, but—with fish?"

"I like it with everything."

"Nobody will come to arrest us?"

"If they do, I'll protect you."

158

The waiter poured, and Tom raised his glass. Sarah followed.

"To a future," Tom said softly, "of warm evenings on the water, picnics in Gloucester, nonmicrowave dinners . . . and expertly polished toenails."

"Don't forget ever-taller buildings with you standing out on top."

Annoyance clouded his features, but he pushed it back determinedly and sipped the wine.

"It's delicious," Sarah said.

The band was playing a slow song, and the seductive melody wound around them. Tom stood and took Sarah's hand to lead her to the floor. She fitted into his arms as if she'd been there in an earlier life, and they moved to the sweet tune almost as one person.

Tom ran his hands down Sarah's bare, smooth back. Her lilac halter dress had intrigued him from the moment she'd greeted him at her door tonight, and when he'd seen it was backless, he couldn't wait to get his hands on her. They were in public, but she was dressed; it was perfectly proper. Something about that turned his pilot light up, as though he had a secret license for pleasure that no one else had.

When the dance was over, he reluctantly released Sarah, except for a hand on her waist to guide her back to the table. His dark gray Brooks Brothers suit, his best, was a bit damp. Being that close to her tended to heat him up, especially on a night that was warm to begin with. Well . . . he intended for it to get even warmer later.

159

They ate oysters on the half shell and had some more wine. A basket of warm corn sticks arrived, with a little pot of sweet butter, and they each devoured two.

"Good opportunity to work those off," Tom said when the band moved into a fast number, and they went back to the floor.

The harbor breeze and the music were so pleasant, they danced for some time before Tom realized that his knee hurt. He was tempted to keep going; it felt as if it would probably hold out a good while yet. But he decided not to push his luck. The prospect of being incapacitated again was hateful enough to make him cautious. He spoke in Sarah's ear, and they went back to the table.

"That was fun," she said, holding out her glass for wine.

"For me too. I wouldn't have stopped, except that my knee started to hurt."

"Oh, Tom, no! How bad is it?"

"Not bad at all. It's nothing."

"Is that the truth?"

"Of course. Forget it."

Their entrées came, scallops for Sarah and shrimp scampi for Tom. In a nice piece of timing the band took a break then and returned just as they were finishing their coffee.

"Come on," Tom said, holding her chair.

"You don't mean you want to dance?"

"Well, I wasn't planning to walk off with this chair."

"You can't dance."

160

"Thanks a lot. Are you saying I have two left feet?"

"No, Tom." She folded her arms. "I'm saying you have an injured knee."

"Oh, can it, Sarah. I *had* an injured knee for three weeks. It's fine now. I just had a twinge before, that's all. And this is a slow song."

"No."

"I don't believe this," he said. "Get out of that chair and dance with me."

"Don't you dare—"

He grabbed her arm and pulled her to her feet. "You're confused. I'm going to straighten you out." His eyes bored into hers. She rubbed the spot where his fingers had been. "You're not my shrink, my doctor, or a caretaker of any kind. You're the woman I love."

"Well, of course! Just because I'm concerned about your knee—"

"You love being concerned! It's your hobby! You love it more than you love me—and I'm sick of it!"

"That's ridiculous, Tom," Sarah said hotly. "You're being a macho jackass. I just don't want you to hurt yourself again. I want you to keep making progress."

"For the last time, Sarah—*my* progress is *my* business. Leave it to me!"

It was off his chest now. Tom looked at Sarah's angry, hurt face, and his fury ebbed.

"Look," he said, stroking her arm where he'd grabbed it, "I just don't need more help, you know?" He pulled her close. "Now I want to dance."

161

Sarah was tempted to argue again but closed her mouth before she could say anything. Clearly he intended to dance; there was nothing she could do about it.

Probably his frustration over the knee was the real cause of his outburst just now. She had to try not to feel insulted; he was letting off steam over a problem that must torment him. A man so active in work and everything else—it must drive him crazy that he didn't have one hundred percent use of his leg.

Well, if he was too busy proving how fine he was to take proper care of his knee, she'd just have to be vigilant for him. It would be up to her to see he didn't overdo it.

"Pagano."

"Hi, it's me."

He smiled. "Hi, me. I was just thinking about last night."

"Thinking what?"

"That—that it was a great evening."

"It was. I had a good time."

"Sorry you couldn't stay the whole night."

Sarah smiled into the phone. "Me too. If only I could teach Lily to feed herself sometimes. How's your knee?"

Irritation bit at him. In fact, he'd lied when he said he was thinking that they'd had a great evening. He'd been remembering his lecture and trying to decide how much of it had penetrated. She'd said a few things later that had made him wonder, as he was wondering now, with a sinking feeling that got worse by the minute.

"It's fine. Did I tell you how nice you looked? That backless dress was dynamite."

"Thanks. I have another one something like it in yellow."

"I'll have to give you an opportunity to wear it."

She laughed. "Your place or mine?"

"I was thinking of something along the lines of Harbor House. So I can dance with you again and maul you legally in public."

"Great. As soon as your knee is all better."

"Sarah—"

"In fact, I know the perfect place," she went on, having missed the warning in his tone. "The Bay Tower Room, on top of the State Street Bank Building. It has dancing and a fabulous view of the harbor. And the neat part is—the building's around sixty stories. So it would be great practice for you. They don't let anyone outside, but it would be interesting to see how you react to spending an evening at that height with all those windows."

The sinking feeling was now such a big hunk of fury that he could say nothing except, "Have to run, I have another call." If he hadn't hung up, he would have blasted her into the middle of next week.

. He slammed his closed fist on the desk, once, twice, three times. Then he got up and stalked out, leaving his secretary staring after him in surprise.

That was it. He wouldn't take any more. He felt

choked with rage and just the leading edge of a sadness bigger than Canada.

Sarah looked at her desk clock and was surprised to see that it was already one-thirty. What had happened to Tom?

She'd called him at his office yesterday to tell him the good news—she'd secured the MacDougall Beverages account, a big, big one she'd been after for months. He wasn't in, but she'd left a message to call and that she was free at noon today. They'd been making it a habit to meet a couple of times a week for lunch.

She was only now noticing that she hadn't heard from him—either yesterday or this morning.

Well, there was just one explanation for that. He must not have gotten the message. Madelyn was conscientious, but everybody slipped sometimes.

"Pagano Construction."

"Hi, this is Sarah Foster. Is he in?"

"No, Ms. Foster, he's out to lunch."

So much for the chance of meeting today. She'd hoped they could get together, even if it was late.

She left another message to call and went downstairs to get a sandwich. The afternoon turned busy after that, with phone calls and applicants coming in, and it was five-fifteen before she thought of Tom again.

She stared at her clock. Something was definitely awry. For a ridiculous moment she wondered if it was broken, running fast for some reason; but she realized immediately that that was nonsense. The going-home sounds filtering in from the rest of the office affirmed that the time was correct, even if she could make herself believe that an electric clock she'd relied on for years was capable of skipping several hours.

A burr of anxiety began to form. It was one of those feelings that you don't want to pursue, because a primeval survival sense warns you that it will lead to much, much worse . . . but you have no choice.

She held it off for a minute, the way you do when you wake in the morning and keep the door closed against a lousy memory from the night before. But she wasn't even a bit asleep now, and she couldn't stop reality from flooding in.

She swallowed the sick dread that started to rise and forced herself to think. It wasn't very likely that Madelyn would fail to give Tom *two* messages, so there went that theory.

But . . . what if she'd forgotten to give him yesterday's? That would cut nearly a full day out of the delay to be accounted for. If he didn't get the first message, then for all practical purposes she hadn't called until one-thirty today. And if he'd gone to a construction site right from lunch and hadn't yet phoned his office, he still might not know she wanted to reach him.

That could very well be it. Sarah let out the breath she hadn't realized she'd been holding.

Of course, there was another possibility. Something might have happened on a job this afternoon —another accident or a phobic problem. It was unlikely—but then, so was the chance of Tom not calling her back.

There was only one way to settle this. With a finger that was just starting to tremble she dialed his office. The phone rang five times, then six, and disappointment rose. The service would answer, and they wouldn't know—

"Pagano Construction," a breathless Madelyn said.

Sarah sagged in relief. "This is Sarah Foster. I—"

"Oh, Ms. Foster. You just caught me. I had to unlock the door again—that was what took me so long."

"I was just wondering if—if Tom was in," Sarah said, knowing as she asked that he wouldn't be, not if Madelyn was locking up.

"No. He left about fifteen minutes ago. Didn't he call you back?"

"No," Sarah almost whispered. Then, hating herself, she said, "I left a message yesterday too. Do you know if he got that one?"

"Yes. Definitely," the woman said a little testily. "I always give him his messages."

"I know. I'm sorry. Thank you."

Sarah hung up and clasped her hands on the desk. They felt oddly cold and shivery. She tried to take a deep breath to calm herself, but the effort to inhale over the hurt in her chest was huge.

A sensible voice asked, What's the tragedy? So he didn't return a couple of calls. Maybe he's busy. It isn't like you to go all unglued over a small unexplained thing.

But her instinctual side knew better. It recalled niggles of questions she'd felt recently, a sense that things weren't quite right. Not like before Tom's

166

accident when she'd been tense and off-kilter; more a shadow of something on Tom's mind, something that had to do with her. Something that —that made it not a complete surprise that he wasn't hurrying to be in touch with her. That he was—face it—avoiding her.

Somehow she got herself home without hitting a tree, a car, or a speed above seventy. She fed Lily, changed her clothes, and wished this horrible day would be over.

But there was another cruel surprise yet to come. It arrived in an eight-thirty call from Vivian at the clinic.

"Sarah," she said, "I'm glad I reached you." Vivian always began her calls that way, as though she'd been dialing you for hours and was about to send out a search party. "What a shame it didn't work out with Tom Pagano. I hope you're not taking it too personally. These things have to be expected, you know, and you're lucky that you've hardly . . ."

Vivian was still talking, but Sarah was a mile behind, trying to figure out what she meant. Though her stomach had jumped at the first words —as though Vivian knew of their real relationship and that something was wrong—there was only one "it" she could be referring to.

"Vivian," she interrupted, "what precisely are you saying?"

"Well, Sarah, only that you have my support and understanding—"

"On what issue, exactly?" A voice in her mind sang, *Notagainnotagainnotagainnotagain.*

167

There was a second of quiet. "On Tom asking for a different aide."

There was silence on Sarah's end now, a shocked moment she couldn't help. He wasn't dropping out of the workshop again. It was worse.

Vivian might have been an idiot, but she was still a psychologist. She said, "Sarah, don't tell me this is the first you've heard?"

"Yes," she said. What was the point?

"Oh, not this again. I thought we made it clear the first time he acted without talking to his aide that this was not the way we structure the program. Perhaps you can give him a call and—"

"No."

"Pardon?"

"I won't call him."

"Sarah," she coaxed in the tone that always made Sarah think Cajoling 101 had been a required course for her doctorate, "I understand that you feel hurt and threatened, but—"

"I won't call him."

"Well. If you feel that strongly about it."

Sarah said, "I couldn't feel more strongly if he'd sent me a letter bomb."

She hung up and took Lily in her arms and cried into the soft fur.

CHAPTER TEN

Sarah was at her kitchen window, watching the sun set, when she saw the yellow Toyota pull in.

"Oh, no," she said aloud, though there was no one to hear but Lily.

If she'd ever wanted company less, she couldn't recall when. Her evenings—the five that had passed since Vivian's call—were lonely, but she was still too depressed to do anything other than endure them. She had to rejoin the living sooner or later; eventually she'd start to get herself out, see friends. But not yet; she couldn't yet.

The worst part was, she should have known this could happen. She should never have left herself in a position to be mowed down. Once before, when things got too itchy, he'd dropped out; it didn't take Freud to see that he'd be likely to do that again, in a bigger way this time. She'd known all along that Tom's ego was tender where the phobia was concerned. It should be no shock that the man couldn't stand showing his "weakness" to the woman he loved, let alone work with her on it.

Well, she hadn't been prepared, that was all.

Whatever she'd known, however deeply she'd known it, she'd preferred to keep it buried.

So now you pay the price for letting your heart carry you where your mind should at least have shared the trip, she thought as she watched her grandmother lock the car. Empty nights, a shaky, chilled feeling that never went away . . . and the frustration of being trapped like a bottled firefly when people who had no idea expected you to act like yourself. She didn't know how she'd get through this. Having to pretend at work that everything was fine was hard enough; she doubted she could string her grandmother along for six seconds.

The bell rang. Sarah steeled herself and opened the door.

"Hi, dear," Jan said. "Busy?"

"No," Sarah said, wondering, *Would she leave if I said yes?*

Jan peered at her face. "What's the matter?"

"Nothing. I—don't feel too well."

"Poor dear. Can I help?"

Don't be kind to me when I'm wishing you away. I can't stand it. "No. I'll be okay. Come on in."

"I have a little something that might make you feel better."

A cyanide capsule would be nice.

"It's in the car. Come out and help me carry it."

Oh, no, Sarah thought. Something big. And no Tom to take it away to his den this time. Jan was walking ahead of her across the parking lot and didn't see her squeeze back tears.

170

"It's in here," Jan said, opening the trunk. She raised the lid.

Sarah stared at the thing, a big cylindrical object with a crank. She hadn't the remotest—

"It's an old-fashioned ice-cream freezer," Jan said. She handed Sarah a paper bag. "Stick this under your arm. It's rock salt. Now, if you lift here and I—"

"I can take it myself," Sarah said. They went inside, and Sarah set the freezer in a corner of the kitchen floor.

"Put it on the table. I'll show you what to do. It really works, and it'll make the best ice cream you ever ate. You'll have to go to the library and check an old cookbook for the exact ingredients, but I can—"

Sarah said, "I, really—I'm afraid I can't use this."

Jan turned to look at her.

"I'm sorry. I know you went to trouble to get it for me, but . . . you must *know* I have no use for an ice-cream maker. I keep telling you I don't like to have fattening things around. And there's no room for it."

The hurt and, worse, understanding in the old woman's clear gray eyes pierced Sarah like an arrow.

"I wish you'd tell me what's wrong," Jan said quietly.

Sarah turned away. She dug her nails into her palms. Why, *why* had her grandmother chosen this of all times to trot in another white elephant? She couldn't deal with it; she had no control left.

171

The strain of keeping her heart from shattering into bits had used it all up.

"What's wrong," she choked out, "is that I'm tired of you bringing me things! What do you expect me to do with all these useless eyesores that nobody wants?" She was silent for a horrified moment before bursting into tears.

Her grandmother took a chair and waited patiently while Sarah's sobs grew and then began to subside.

"When you were small," she said, "you wouldn't let anyone comfort you when you cried. You're too old for me to try that now. And you're certainly too old not to be held accountable for saying hurtful things to your doddering old grandmother."

"I know," Sarah said, sniffling. "I'm so sorry."

"You may think I'm just silly and vague, but I'm a real person with feelings. Feelings you've tramped on."

"Please," Sarah said, "stop. You're right—everything you're saying is right. I deserve it. But I-I've had enough."

"I assume you don't mean . . . enough suits of armor."

She shook her head. Her brown hair was damp around her face, and it got wetter as she wiped tears back from her cheeks.

"Well," Jan asked, reaching over to thumb a stray drop from Sarah's chin, "do you want to talk about whatever has you in such a dither, or would you rather I left?" Sarah started to answer and she said, "Wait. I withdraw the question. You needn't talk if you don't want to, but I don't care to leave just yet. Maybe after you've calmed down."

Sarah said, "You shouldn't be so nice to me when I've been so rotten."

Jan said, "You're right."

Sarah went to the window and rested her arms on the sill. Her nose touched the screen with its odd, grimy-metallic smell that nothing but a window screen ever has. Tiger Lily gazed placidly at her from the stove where she sat near the part that covered the pilot light.

It was nearly dark. She couldn't see much. A small car came into the lot, parked, and doused its lights. A chain jingled, and the silhouettes of a spaniel and a man went by.

"What's the matter is Tom," she said without turning. "He doesn't want to see me anymore."

"Good heavens. Why?"

"I don't know. He didn't bother to say."

"Well, what do you *think* went wrong?"

"I think . . . I knew him too well. I mean, he thought I did. He couldn't handle having his girlfriend and his phobia aide be the same person."

"Why not?"

"Because it was threatening, I guess. Like having someone see you with your teeth out."

"Nice of you to use a comparison I can relate to," Jan said dryly.

"Oh, Grandma." Sarah sat at the table. "I didn't mean anything like that."

She patted Sarah's hand. "I was joking. So this nice man with the tan and the muscles was too embarrassed to keep dating a magnificent young

173

woman just because she knew about his difficulty?"

"Yes. At least, that's the only explanation I can come up with. Otherwise, why wouldn't he have had the nerve to face me? Something had been on his mind, I could see that, but he didn't say a word. He just dropped out of my life." She explained about the unreturned calls, the message from Vivian. "And we were so close." She rubbed her eyes. "I loved him. I guess I still do. And he loved me, I know he did. But he couldn't stick with it. His ego was too fragile."

Jan raised her eyebrows. "Didn't you tell me when you first started climbing buildings with him that he was mean? Rude?"

"Yes. He was dictatorial. Even after he got to know me and stopped being nasty, he always wanted things his way."

"And wasn't shy about saying so."

"No. Never."

Jan shrugged. "That doesn't sound like a tender ego to me. It sounds like a very strong, secure man who knows what he wants and insists on having it."

"He wasn't strong and secure about his phobia. It embarrassed him."

"Well, naturally. Didn't yours you? Why else did I have to render you instantly pregnant in the elevator that day? No, Sarah," she said firmly, getting up and opening a cabinet, "just because a big macho man is ashamed that he fears heights doesn't mean he can't bear for anyone to know him as he really is. There must be more to this.

174

Look a little further. Change directions, perhaps. Consider what *you* were after."

Sarah noticed that Jan was poking through her cabinets. "What are you looking for?"

"Tea. I thought I'd make us some. You could use it." She studied her granddaughter, small and sad at the kitchen table. "On second thought, I think not." She closed the cabinets. "Where do you keep your liquor? Oh, I remember." She went into the living room and returned with a bottle of vodka. She poured some over ice in two glasses, added about a thimbleful of tonic to each, gave Sarah one, and raised hers.

"To my granddaughter, the fighter," she said. "Drink up, dear."

Something flickered in Sarah's mind—a fragment of recollection—and then died.

"Fighter? Me?" she said. "Ha."

"Nonsense. You are definitely a class-A fighter. You inherited it from me."

"But I've always been a cream puff in so many ways."

"Small ways. And you fight to get out from under those, like you did with your elevator problem. Nobody can be completely strong all the time."

Sarah sipped her drink. "You are."

"I most certainly am not. I'm strong where it counts—you'll never see me give up and go to Florida, that graveyard for the victims of life—but I have my needs. It's inhuman not to."

"You're just trying to make me feel better. What do you need besides garage sales?"

175

Her grandmother gazed at her. "I need you to need me to go to them," she said softly.

Sarah clasped her arms around her middle and bowed her head.

"No," Jan said, "don't feel bad. You were rude and you apologized, and that's that. The rest isn't your responsibility; it's mine. I need to be depended on for something. But I didn't tell you that so you'd feel guilty. I said it to make a point. Well," she said, standing, "I'd better go before I have any more of this drink. It'll do you good to finish yours *and* mine, anyway. I'm leaving while I can still drive."

Sarah walked her out and they hugged. She came back into the kitchen, looked at the two drinks, shrugged, and emptied Jan's glass into hers. She took it into the living room and curled up on the couch. Lily came in and jumped up, meowing for attention.

She scratched behind the pointy ears with one hand and lifted her glass with the other. Again something pricked her memory, as it had in the kitchen when her grandmother toasted her.

What was knocking at her mental door? Maybe if she closed her eyes and let her memories drift . . .

But that was dangerous. It was exactly what caused Tom to wander in, when what she should be doing more of was canceling him out. Not letting her recollections remind her of how she hurt.

She took another sip of the drink. It had long since lost its fizz, if there had ever been enough tonic in it to produce any, but she felt soothed. The vodka was making her languid and drowsy. Her grandmother had good instincts. Left to her own devices, she probably wouldn't have had anything —maybe just coffee or a glass of wine.

Wine.

There was that prickle again.

She stroked Lily's back and scratched her good by the tail, the way she liked it. The cat arched toward Sarah and purred deafeningly.

She and Tom had had wine at Harbor House, and he'd made a toast that night. Remembering, she almost cried again. What had they drunk to? Evenings on the water, picnics . . . nonmicrowave dinners . . . and there were a couple of other things.

Now her body was remembering, too, tingling at the recollection of his big bed, the love they'd shared there. Tom in his shorts . . . and out of them. The awkward immobilizer, the way he hadn't let it interfere with his desire. How wonderful his arms felt, his hands pressing her to him . . . his mouth all over her.

That was what he'd said in the toast—polished toenails. She thought back, summoning the feel of his fingers on her toes, his lips there . . . everything he'd said. He'd told her that her feet were as gorgeous as the rest of her.

Had he set out to torture her deliberately? What kind of man, she asked the silence, loves you all over, including your toes . . . says only the most adoring things . . . can't be with you enough—and then decides he can solve what's really *his* problem by pushing *you* away?

Her mind harked back to Harbor House again.

"Don't forget ever-taller buildings," she heard herself saying as they raised their glasses, "with you standing out on top."

She felt a stab deep inside. That was the elusive recollection—the look on Tom's face when she'd said that. She hadn't paid much attention at the time, but she remembered now how angry he'd looked.

Other pictures crowded her mind. Staying at Tom's and taking care of him. How lovely that was. How he couldn't wait to get rid of the immobilizer, but she could have gone on forever, looking after things and helping him out.

The difference between the Tom who was with her in work sessions and the Tom who was just with her.

The way he'd been when she didn't want him to dance. What he'd told her then, so angry that his fingers had left small bruise spots on her arm: "You're not my shrink, my doctor, or a caretaker. . . . You're the woman I love."

For some reason her grandmother intruded, the image of her at the kitchen table. "I need to be depended on."

And Tom again: "Don't *help* so much."

She leapt up from the couch, dumping Lily, who yowled softly in protest. Her head hurt; too much vodka on top of not enough food. But the mental snapshots were making her head hurt, too, for they were forming a mosaic, a big picture that made her hot with shame.

Tom hadn't simply walked out of her life for no

reason. He had a reason, a very logical and important one. It was bad enough that she hadn't seen it, but he'd have forgiven that. No, the awful part was that she hadn't listened when he warned her.

He could have gone on loving her, maybe forever, she saw now. She'd messed that up, muddied the chance with her obtuse unwillingness to see what she was trying to do, even to hear when he told her.

She remembered the odd tension she'd felt before Tom was hurt, when Dr. Doan said she was grinding her teeth. She'd put it down to being in love. Well, that had been a comfy explanation, but it was tripe. She'd been tense because the shoe had changed feet. The balance had shifted between her and Tom. By then she was needier than he was.

She paced the living room, rubbing her head. Lily watched from the couch. She'd begun to relax after Tom's accident—after the balance had swung again and she was needed once more. And when he'd mended, she did her best to keep the dependency alive.

She groaned in the quiet room, remembering the things she'd said . . . how she'd kept focusing on his fear, his injury . . . long after those should have taken a backseat to the beautiful thing they'd built. Long after all he'd wanted was to love her and have her love him back.

Sarah found a spot two blocks from the Revere Tower and backed into it. She hadn't seen the Pontiac parked, but it wasn't easy to find a space around Copley Square. He could be on any one of several side streets.

In any case, he'd be up there waiting—waiting for Lisa Masters, his new aide.

Her hands felt moist as she raised the windows and shut off the engine. She hoped what she was about to do would achieve the end she prayed for. But he might be furious. Maybe she'd ruin any small chance they had of getting back together—when all she wanted was that.

For the fiftieth time she wondered if she should have just called or gone to see him in Salem. And once more her instincts told her no. He could hang up a phone; he could pretend not to be home. On top of a seventy-story building he was a captive audience. He had to hear her out.

She'd phoned Lisa yesterday, the day after her long, painful self-examination, to find out how Tom was progressing. She was trying to decide how to approach him. When she'd learned that Tom was about to do his "graduation" exercise—going out on the tallest building in the city—she'd known at once that this was her chance. She'd taken the older woman into her confidence, and Lisa had reluctantly agreed to let Sarah meet Tom in her place.

She locked the car and started toward the building. The hot wind caught her hair; it stuck in her lipstick and she brushed it away. Now that she was actually about to see him, talk to him, her knees felt feeble.

She rode up in the elevator. She'd tried to accept that he still might not want to see her, no matter how much explaining she did; in all the time she'd been with him, Tom had always been certain of what he wanted, committed to his decisions. But she hadn't really succeeded. She didn't know how she'd bear it if he still didn't want her.

There was a wild moment when she got off the elevator during which she wanted nothing more than to step into the one just going down. Suddenly not having to face Tom seemed much better than discovering he didn't love her, wouldn't ever again.

But she made herself go straight to the bank of doors that led out to the observation deck. She'd come this far; she'd go all the way if it took every ounce of strength she wished she had.

There weren't many people outside. The strong breeze on the ground was a powerful wind seventy stories up—not the nicest sort of day for enjoying the view. But there was Tom over by the high wall, leaning on it and looking out over the city.

Again the urge to run away almost overtook her. In a few minutes she might have no fantasies, no hopeful illusions left. The profile that was so dearly familiar—she could see the line of his full lower lip, the flash of sun on his aviator glasses—might be lost to her forever. His solid body, the muscular arms that could cradle her with love or grip her urgently . . . maybe she'd never feel them again.

But once more she made herself plunge ahead. "Tom?" she said from behind him.

He didn't turn. Her heart lurched. Then she

realized that he probably couldn't hear in the wind.

"Tom," she said again, louder.

Her hair blew across her eyes. She pushed it back just as he turned.

She watched his face and wanted to die when she saw it freeze.

"Sarah," he said. "What are you doing here?"

For a minute she couldn't do anything but gaze with pain and longing at the strong, tanned face that was in her dreams every night, her thoughts all day.

"Sarah?" he repeated, impatient for her to answer.

She found herself staring at his neck, the fragrant skin she'd snuggled into on so many lovely nights . . . the sprinkle of beard that was so exciting against her cheek.

"I took Lisa's place," she said, trying to sound brisk and confident but not succeeding. He leaned nearer to hear her better, and the bittersweet agony of having him so close was unbearable. "I had to come. I . . ." Her throat was closing as tears threatened. She turned away so he wouldn't see.

She'd been alone for so long, cherishing her hard-won independence; but in the months she'd known Tom, that had changed. She'd grown used to having caring arms to comfort her. Their absence was so stark now. She stood with her back to him, trying to keep control, but she missed the balm of his hug so much, it was like being deprived of a part of herself. To have him right there, close enough to touch her but unwilling to, was torture.

She didn't want to face him. She yearned to put off the confrontation still longer. As bad as it was not to know for sure how he felt, to hear the worst would be excruciating. But she had to find the courage. She had to do this; she had to settle it.

She turned. His face was still set in the grim, defensive lines it had taken on as soon as he'd seen her instead of Lisa.

"Why did you have to come?" he asked.

The question was so harsh, she felt sick. Unconsciously she put a hand to her stomach. She was trying to find an answer when he seemed to realize that in trying to be heard over the wind he'd sounded rougher than he meant to.

"I mean," he said, "what were you going to say? You told me a minute ago you had to come."

"I had to explain," she said.

"Explain what?"

"I think I know why you stopped seeing me."

His expression didn't change, but he took a step back. Sarah hadn't expected that; it demolished what was left of her nerve. The smallest encouragement would have kept her going, but if he was backing away from her, there was nothing further to do. He was showing her that he didn't want to hear any more. She still had to look at herself in the mirror, and she wouldn't be able to if she made a bigger jerk of herself than she had already. With a last look at the face she adored she turned and walked back toward the doors.

She was concentrating so hard on keeping herself intact, at least until she got to her car, that she didn't realize that Tom had followed until he gripped her shoulder. He turned her around.

"Where are you going?" he asked, and let go.

She made herself ignore the heated imprint from his touch. "I didn't think you wanted me to say anything else."

"What?" he asked, leaning closer.

"Do you want to listen to me or not?"

He nodded once. "Let's have it."

If she let herself hesitate . . . wonder if he was just humoring her . . . think about how much more humiliated she could still feel . . . she'd never get it out.

"I'm sorry," she said. "I wish I'd listened when you told me what I was doing. I wish it hadn't taken me so long to come to my senses. I didn't realize . . . I didn't see until it all came crashing down. How I tried to make you keep needing me." Tears spilled out, wetting her flying hair. She pushed the whole mess away.

For the longest moment of her life he simply stared. Then his face changed as if he'd pulled off a hardened covering.

"Oh, Sarah," he said. His words were a moan. She felt his arms around her, his lips in her hair. Her tears flowed, wetting his shirt.

"I'm so glad you came," he said in her ear, "so glad. I went for broke. I was frantic. I thought I'd lost you." He tightened his grip.

She pulled back. "You thought you'd lost *me?*"

She looked so helplessly puzzled that he had to smile, though he could only force a small one past the feelings that were crowding in. "I wanted you

184

to just be *you*—not my permanent rock," he said. "When I couldn't make you see that, I took the chance that you'd be shocked into figuring it out yourself if I stepped aside. But, God, it was hard. I hated to do it. I hated being without you."

Holding her hair out of her face, Sarah looked at him. So he'd never meant for it to be over! He was anxious for them to get back together too!

"You mean—you were hoping I'd come to you?" she asked.

"Hoping?" he repeated, his eyes dark and hungry. "I prayed for it. There was nothing on earth I wanted more than to have you with me again."

"Then why did you—why did I have to—"

"Sarah, don't you get it? It had to be you. *You* had to realize what was happening with us. *You* had to want to make it different. I tried, and you wouldn't hear."

Through her tumble of emotions Sarah knew that he was right. Though it had hurt so when he'd abruptly rejected what they had, he'd done it for both of them; brought them pain in the hope of saving their love. She understood now. They had to start again from a different place—one where the clinic, and their roles in it, didn't exist.

"The workshop—the whole business—is done," she said. "The first thing I'm going to do is forget you were ever in it."

"Not yet. Before you do, enjoy this with me—all of this and everything it means." He swept an arm around her. "For all the trouble it caused between us—and I was pretty impossible myself—I still have to thank you for the fact that I'm up here. So look around, feel good and proud—and then we'll put this behind us and be what I think you want as much as I do—two people who love each other."

"I want that more than anything," Sarah said.

Tom reached for her, and there was an instant of soaring joy when she knew for sure that she hadn't lost it, the heaven of his arms. Then he was holding her, clasping her against his chest, his hands moving over her possessively, as if to make up for the time lost.

He touched his lips to hers in an electric homecoming. From far down where feeling begins, a moan rose from her, a sound of happiness rediscovered. She pressed as close to him as she could and let bliss settle over her.

Now you can reserve March's
Candlelights
before they're published!

💜 You'll have copies set aside for *you*
   the instant they come off press.
💜 You'll save yourself precious shopping
   time by arranging for *home delivery*.
💜 You'll feel proud and efficient about
   organizing a system that *guarantees* delivery.
💜 You'll avoid the disappointment of not
   finding *every* title you want and need.

ECSTASY SUPREMES $2.75 each

- [ ] **113 NIGHT STRIKER**, A. Lorin 16391-9-12
- [ ] **114 THE WORLD IN HIS ARMS**, J. Brandon 19767-8-12
- [ ] **115 RISKING IT ALL**, C. Murray 17446-5-23
- [ ] **116 A VERY SPECIAL LOVER**, E. Elliott 19315-X-27

ECSTASY ROMANCES $2.25 each

- [ ] **410 SWEET-TIME LOVIN'**, B. Cameron 18419-3-24
- [ ] **411 SING SOFTLY TO ME**, D. Phillips 17865-7-33
- [ ] **412 ALL A MAN COULD WANT**, L.R. Wisdom 10179-4-39
- [ ] **413 SOMETHING WILD AND FREE**, H. Conrad . . . 18134-8-10
- [ ] **414 TO THE HIGHEST BIDDER**, N. Beach 18707-9-33
- [ ] **415 HANDS OFF THE LADY**, E. Randolph 13427-7-17
- [ ] **416 WITH EVERY KISS**, S. Paulos 19744-9-28
- [ ] **417 DREAM MAKER**, D.K. Vitek 12155-8-17

At your local bookstore or use this handy coupon for ordering:

DELL READERS SERVICE—DEPT. B952A
P.O. BOX 1000, PINE BROOK, N.J. 07058

Please send me the above title(s). I am enclosing $_____(please add 75¢ per copy to cover postage and handling). Send check or money order—no cash or COD's. Please allow 3-4 weeks for shipment.
CANADIAN ORDERS: please submit in U.S. dollars.

Ms Mrs Mr _____

Address_____

City State_____ Zip _____

Rebels and outcasts, they fled halfway across the earth to settle the harsh Australian wastelands. Decades later—ennobled by love and strengthened by tragedy—they had transformed a wilderness into fertile land. And themselves into

The Australians

WILLIAM STUART LONG

THE EXILES, #1	12374-7-12	$3.95
THE SETTLERS, #2	17929-7-45	$3.95
THE TRAITORS, #3	18131-3-21	$3.95
THE EXPLORERS, #4	12391-7-29	$3.95
THE ADVENTURERS, #5	10330-4-40	$3.95
THE COLONISTS, #6	11342-3-21	$3.95

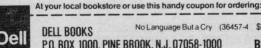